Sharpe Turn: Murder by the Book

Cozy Suburbs Mysteries, Volume 4

Lisa B. Thomas

Published by Lisa B. Thomas, 2016.

Copyright

SHARPE TURN: MURDER BY THE BOOK

Prologue

No wonder women in Texas have such big hair. Her stylist used more aerosol hairspray in this one sitting than the entire line of Rockettes would use in a whole stage show. Alexis Dekker stared at her reflection in the rearview mirror as she raced back to her house on Battle Bend Road.

Obviously, these hillbillies in Maycroft had no idea how to do hair. This was her third attempt to get a decent cut and style since she and Max moved here three months ago, and it would definitely be her last. She didn't care what it cost; she would be flying back to the city to let Daphne do her hair from now on. Max would just have to get over it.

Besides, it would give her an excuse to leave these hicks for a few days a month and soak up some of her beloved New York—not to mention all the shopping she could do.

Unfortunately, Maycroft was east of Dallas and quite a distance from the airport. She would get a car to pick her up. Yes, that would work. She hated driving anyway. In the city, she had always taken cabs.

Ahhh. But she did love the smell of rich leather. She ran her hands around the steering wheel of the new pearl red Audi Coupe and took in a deep breath. She veered onto the small road that led to the northeast side of town where her husband had chosen a secluded ranch-style home for their retirement bungalow.

Retirement. Like a writer had anything to retire from. All he did most days was lock himself inside his study and pound away on the keyboard. When they lived in the city, at least they'd go out to dinner in the evening with friends. Now that they had moved to Nowheres-ville, Texas, they ate at home. Luckily, Max did most of the cooking. He knew better than to expect her to do much more than fix the occasional sandwich or pour wine.

Her husband had convinced her to sell their New York City apartment. Alexis had protested but finally had given in. After all, she had plenty of friends to stay with when she visited. Besides, Max wouldn't be around forever. He had a strong will but a weak heart. When the time came to bury him six feet under, she'd be looking down from a penthouse in Manhattan.

Her headlights shone on a pothole up ahead, but she was going too fast to swerve around it. The small car jolted, and she bounced around, hitting her head on the side window. The wine fridge lying in the back seat rattled with the jarring motion of the car.

Alexis cursed the stupid rural town with its winding roads and overgrown pastures and reached for the side of her head where a bump had already begun to form. She glanced back over her shoulder, trying to see if the wine refrigerator had ripped the leather car seat. When she turned back around, the looming tree grew larger against the dusky sky, like a vicious serpent reaching out its tentacles to grab her. The ancient oak was a sentinel, ready to claim anyone who dared to challenge the road's wicked curve. She slammed on her brakes.

It was too late.

She covered her face with both arms, her hands balled into fists. She sucked in her breath and squinted her eyes as tight as possible, bracing herself for the impact.

One lone survivor. A bottle of red wine, left in the trunk from a previous shopping trip, rolled across the pavement amongst the rubble and debris, coming to rest intact against the base of the old tree.

Chapter 1

Compared to a conspiracy, a knife fight, and multiple broken bones, Deena Sharpe's latest problem was small potatoes. After all, she had survived a lot worse circumstances this past year. But in light of her cozy life in her cozy town, this was huge. A Texas-sized showdown was brewing in the Sharpe family, and she was determined to come out the winner.

The titles on the spines of the library books blurred as she craned her neck to read those on the top shelf. If only she were taller. Not freakishly tall, but more than her five-feet-five inches. Gary was over six feet. He could see and reach all the high shelves. Too bad he was at work.

Maybe if she knew what she was looking for, the chore wouldn't feel so tortuous. For whatever reason, this was her blind spot, and the all-too-familiar wave of discouragement began to drown her optimism.

Her toes strained at the ends of her loafers to keep her pushed up long enough to read the titles. As she pulled down a thick tome with a colorful cover, dust drifted through the air and brought on a powerful sneeze.

That was enough. At her feet lay a stack of cookbooks she'd already pulled from the library shelves. Would she uncover the magic bullet buried somewhere inside to conquer this upcoming challenge?

Her blood boiled at the thought of last December when Gary's mother threw down a proverbial gauntlet, which in this case was more like an oven mitt. And, it had been *oh-so* public. The entirety of the Sharpe family had come from places far and wide to gather as one in Deena's little house in the suburbs. It was the Christmas festivity she had long dreaded. No one seemed to care that she'd just gotten out of the hospital and had saved Estelle's life. The only thing the Sharpes seemed to care about was that the food came from Molly's Homestyle Café and not from her own kitchen. Was she really supposed to cook after all that?

Of the many hats Deena had worn throughout the years——wife, sister, teacher, reporter—"hostess" was the one that never quite fit. It was the hat that would slip to the side, teeter, and then fall straight to the ground.

Her mother-in-law was eighty-two going on fifty. It wasn't that she *acted* fifty; it was that she was *stuck* in the fifties. If a woman back then didn't have an inner-June Cleaver, there was something wrong with her. Deena was too progressive for the elder Mrs. Sharpe. Gary's sister was a natural. And she had kids. Deena and Gary had not been able to have children. Still not an excuse.

Scooping up the books, she trudged along like "dead chef walking" toward the front desk. Cooking. She needed help and she knew it. Wasn't acceptance the first step to recovery?

She plopped the stack on the counter and stared into the cold, dark eyes of librarian Betty Donaldson. "Hi. I'm Deena. And I can't cook."

Betty snickered as she read some of the titles. "*How to Cook Anything. Mealtime for Beginners. No-Brainer Baking.*"

Deena's chin dropped to her chest. "I know. It's pitiful to be pushing sixty and have to admit I can't do something that others consider a no-brainer." Sure, she was being overly dramatic, even pathetic. She didn't care. That's how she felt.

Betty robotically scanned the barcodes into the computer. "So, why now?"

Deena hesitated. Betty was probably thinking, *you can't teach an old dog new tricks.* Maybe she was an old dog, but she was teachable. Hadn't she learned to ride a horse at thirty-five? Hadn't she learned to play Sudoku when it was all the rage? Sure, she hated it and quit, but she had learned. She had even mastered Gary's fancy remote control for their new big-screen television.

But cooking was a horse of a different color. "Gary's sixtieth birthday is coming up, and his mother dared me—*dared* me—to try to fix his favorite dessert." She put her hand to her forehead and let out a sigh. "She's never accepted me because I didn't give her grandchildren. I had a hysterectomy at thirty, so she thinks I'm defective." Deena waited for Betty to offer up the obligatory sympathy and tea one would expect.

Nothing.

Deena continued. "So I signed up for a cooking class through the adult education program at the community college." She picked up one of the cookbooks. It smelled like burnt sugar. Not a good sign. "I thought I'd try to do some self-study before the first class tonight." Her head ached from reading all the titles. How was she going to handle reading the insides?

Betty peered over black reading glasses. "You realize that cooking and baking are two different beasts, right?"

"It's all a black art to me. I might as well be trying to rebuild a car engine or paint the ceiling of the Sistine Chapel."

"That's been done, so you're off the hook for that one." Betty walked over to shush some teenagers laughing too loudly by the computers.

Cooking was an art. *The Art of Cooking*. That was one of the cookbooks she'd left on the shelf. Sure, she could throw some ingredients in a pan and heat them up, but that wasn't the same thing. She eyed the books as though they were weapons of mass destruction.

Betty returned to the eagle's perch.

"Nobody criticizes you if you can't play the piano or sing an aria, so why is it so humiliating if you can't cook?" Deena asked. "It's a talent, right?"

Betty arched an unplucked eyebrow and huffed out an unsympathetic groan. She was close to retirement age and looked every bit the part of the spinster town librarian. Except, she was married and hated cats. A sly grin belied her amusement at Deena's plight as she thumbed through some of the pages of one of the books.

"I'm an untalented failure." Deena crossed her arms on the counter and dropped her head. She was looking for support but had come to the wrong place.

Betty whacked Deena's head with a copy of *Cooking for Dummies*. "Lighten up. I've never seen you so discouraged. I'd be glad to help you, but I can't cook either."

"Really?" Deena sucked in a quick breath, and her spirits rose as she looked up. "But you always bring such nice dishes to our luncheons."

"Two words: Marie Callender's. Check the frozen food aisle."

Relief washed over Deena, but the feeling was short-lived. An image of Mrs. Sylvia Sharpe with her perfectly coifed silver hair and nearly wrinkle-free skin danced in front of her face. For such an old woman, she showed no mercy when she threw down the dessert challenge like a WWE wrestler. Then it hit her. "You know, maybe I don't need to learn a bunch of fancy cooking techniques. I just have to master this one dessert. After all, Gary's mother lives out of state, so we don't see her that often. Plus, she's getting up there in age and—"

"Deena Sharpe! Don't even think like that! Talk about bad karma." Betty crossed herself even though she wasn't Catholic.

At least Deena didn't think she was. She had known Betty for years but couldn't recall her ever mentioning church.

Clamping her mouth shut, Deena pictured her mother-in-law in her "Kiss the Cook" apron and high heels. Actually, that was someone she'd seen on *Mad Men*. "You don't know what it's been like to live under the shadow of Betty Crocker all these years," she protested.

"Uh, I don't? My *name* is Betty. Do you know how many times people call me Betty Crocker?"

Deena had to laugh. "Fair enough. We're tied." She reached for the stack of books. "Maybe I'll just take the ones on baking."

"Good idea." Betty punched on the keyboard and re-scanned the books. Then she pulled off her glasses, leaving them to hang on the gold chain around her neck. "You know who is an excellent cook, don't you?"

"Who?"

"Your neighbor—Christy Ann. I bet she'd be willing to help you."

Deena nearly choked on her own saliva. Of all the people she made an effort to avoid in their small Texas town, Christy Ann was at the top of her list. She was one of the most competitive people Deena had ever met. The woman could turn praying into a competition. "Over my dead body. I don't care if she's the 'Julia Child of Maycroft,' she's the last person I'd ask for help."

"Suit yourself." Betty slid the two baking books across the counter and stacked the others on a cart to be re-shelved.

"I wonder if I can get my money back for the cooking class."

"Here's a thought," Betty said, brightening and straightening her square shoulders. "Why don't you take the Mystery Writing course with me? That's right up your alley. I'm surprised you haven't tried to write one already."

"Mystery writing?" Deena's eyes darted back and forth between Betty and the book-lined shelves. "I must admit that I've thought about it. When I was teaching, I was too busy. Then there was my brief stint at the newspaper..."

"I used to always read your articles. They were a little dry but well written."

Deena's face tightened. "They were *news* stories. They were supposed to be dry." Her claws flared like a mama cat's.

She fished in her purse for her car keys, needing time to think. Writing a novel was an idea she'd toyed with on and off but never seriously considered. Journalist and fiction writers were as different as...well...cooking and baking. It would be hard to make the transition. Still, it might be fun to explore. "I wonder if the class is full already."

"Actually, it is. But I know the gal at the college in charge of enrollment. I could get you in. Besides, there's always at least one person who drops out of these things. I can call her."

Deena faced another watershed moment. Like when Ian Davis asked her to work for him as an investigator. Look how that turned out. She ended up at the wrong end of a sharp blade. Throwing caution to the wind, she agreed. "Sure. It sounds like fun."

Betty rocked back on her heels. "Here's the best part. It's being taught by Max Dekker."

Not quite as famous as John Grisham or James Patterson, Max Dekker had a blockbuster debut novel. He continued to put out hit after hit and just recently moved back to Texas to settle into semi-retirement.

"I saw his name in the course catalog. I couldn't believe such a well-known author would teach a class in our squatty little town."

"Actually, when I heard he and his wife moved to the area, I called my friend at the college and asked her to set up the class. She owed me a favor." Betty jutted out her pointy chin as though taking a dare. "She bugged him so much that he finally gave in."

The wheels turned in Deena's head. Maybe this was it. The thing she'd been looking for to fill the void left by quitting her teaching job and being fired as a reporter. *Deena Sharpe: Mystery Writer.* She liked the way it sounded.

"You missed the first class last Monday, but that's not a problem. Be here tonight at seven o'clock sharp. Should be an interesting class."

Deena chuckled as she tucked the baking books under her arm. "Maybe I'll write one of those cozy mysteries that includes recipes. That'll show Gary's mother he married a good woman.'"

* * *

THE ATTIC IN DEENA'S suburban ranch-style house was stifling hot. In many parts of the country, mid-September meant cool breezes and golden leaves. Not in Northeast Texas. The heat was sticking around like an unwanted guest. Sweat beads dripped in her eyes as she looked for the old metal trunk that housed her childhood memories.

Crazy, the things she chose to keep. Nothing valuable to anyone but her. Most of it was more like trash than treasure.

She spied the trunk she wanted under a stack of tubs filled with Christmas decorations. Getting to it would involve moving other boxes and bins and walking across parts of the attic without flooring. Not worth it. She climbed back down the ladder to the safety of the garage.

What were the chances the short story she had written in high school was worth revisiting anyway? From what she remembered, the main character was a sixteen-year-old girl who wanted to solve the mystery of her missing teacher. It was kids' stuff. Maybe when she had a few real novels under her belt, she would dig the old story out for a good laugh.

This newest endeavor had her antsy. She couldn't wait for Gary to get home to tell him about her day. Hopefully, he wouldn't give her his, "Here we go again" speech. She had heard it much too often lately.

The summer months had passed quickly since her brief stint at the newspaper. She had buried her head in her antique business, occasionally filling in for the owner of the Hidden Treasures Antique Mall. Vacations to Boston and San Francisco were welcome respites from the brutal Texas heat.

The smartest thing she and Gary ever did was put in a backyard pool. Hurley, their rescued terrier, seemed to know it was splash time as soon as he spotted her floral swim towel. Deena led the way to the backyard, and he jumped in the pool before she did.

The silky, cool water was the perfect cleanser for Deena's dusty face. Why couldn't someone invent swimming pool shampoo and conditioner? Then she could kill two birds with one stone.

As usual, Hurley quickly tired of paddling after the tennis ball and jumped out, shaking water all over the deck. He snuggled up next to her towel and flip-flops for a little sun-bathing.

Deena climbed onto a vinyl raft that was slippery with sunscreen. She steadied herself and shooed away a dragonfly attempting to land in her hair. Closing her eyes, she tried to picture Max Dekker. Would he think she and the others in the class were a bunch of corn cob, know-nothings?

After all, Max and his wife had spent most of their time in New York City. Alexis was his literary agent and had made headlines of her own. She was his first and third wife, from what Deena remembered reading. Hard to believe a New York power couple would be happy settling down in Maycroft.

The sun's heat and the soft rocking of the float soon had her drifting off to sleep.

"Hey there," Gary called out.

Deena sat up and tumbled off the raft and into the water. She made her way over to the side of the pool where Gary stood, his tall frame casting a long shadow across the water's ripples.

He sat in a lawn chair and loosened his tie, still a requirement for a financial adviser even in a town where most men wore plaid shirts and cowboy boots.

How was it that his dark hair, sprinkled with gray, was still lying perfectly coifed on his head? It didn't seem fair that he was still in such good shape for a man staring down the barrel of his sixtieth birthday. Deena instinctively sucked in her belly. "I must have dozed off," she said, resting her elbows on the side of the pool.

"Shouldn't you be getting ready? I thought you had that cooking class tonight," Gary said.

"It's not until seven, and it's not cooking anymore. It's writing."

Gary held the tennis ball Hurley had dropped at his feet. "Writing? Would you mind explaining?" He threw the ball.

Deena told him about her visit to the library and the new class she had decided to take. Before he could respond, she said, "And don't lecture me about jumping from one thing to the next. I think this might be the challenge I've been looking for."

Gary hurled the ball to the side fence again, and then picked up the swim towel. "Deena Jo, I've given up questioning your motives." He smiled and tossed her the towel.

Hurley barked then snarled at something on the other side of the wooden fence.

A few seconds later, a door closed.

"Not again," Deena said, the heat rising in her face. "What are we going to do about him?" She pulled the towel tight around her shoulders.

"I don't think there is anything we can do. According to Officer Nelson, he isn't breaking any laws as long as he's on his own side of the fence. Besides, he's harmless."

A chill ran down her spine despite the sun's searing rays. She sneered at Ed Cooper's house next door. "There has to be something we can do. Like put up a second fence so that creeper can't watch us through the slats every time we're out here." She lowered her head and hurried to the back door.

The blast of cold air from inside sent her scurrying to the bedroom to change clothes. When she came out, Gary was working in the kitchen. Hot soup steamed in a saucepan and sandwich fixings covered the counter.

How did she get so lucky to find such a thoughtful husband? The precision with which he assembled the sandwiches was a marvel. She refrained from teasing him about it this time. Never bite the hand that feeds you, right?

"Have you decided what you want for your birthday present?" she asked, snatching a handful of potato chips.

His eyes twinkled. "You know Harvey, the new guy we hired. His wife is making him sell his Harley-Davidson, and I was thinking—"

"Stop right there." She held her hand up. "There's no way you are getting a motorcycle."

"But—"

"I would be worried sick you'd crash and end up in a ditch somewhere. I'm too young to be a widow."

"You're the clumsy one, not me," he protested.

"Does this mean you're having a mid-life crisis?"

He carried the soup bowls to the kitchen table. "Maybe."

"How about something sensible like some nice leather boots or a new set of golf clubs?"

"New clubs?" His eyes twinkled.

Deena bit into her sandwich. "So are you excited about my new venture?"

"You mean *catastrophe*, don't you? Something odd always seems to happen. Just don't wind up in the hospital this time, and it'll be fine."

"Don't worry. This time I'll be writing a mystery, not investigating one."

Chapter 2

The Fitzhugh Library was hopping when Deena arrived unfashionably early. How many budding writers could Maycroft really handle? She looked around for Betty.

Nancy, the other librarian, manned the front desk while parents with their anxious kids waited in line to check out books. It must be science project time at the elementary school.

"Have you seen Betty?" Deena asked when she got to the front of the line.

Nancy cocked her head toward the reading room where some people were starting to gather. "She might be in there. She left before six to get some supper before she had to be back for the class."

The small room held two rows of tables, each with four chairs. Deena chose an empty table at the back and set her satchel in the chair next to her in case Betty wanted to join her. A podium and a tall stool stood ready at the front of the room. A wooden desk sat off to the side near the podium. Chatty women and one man filled several tables in the front.

Someone touched Deena's shoulder, and she jerked around.

"I didn't know you were interested in fiction writing," Lydia Ivey said. "Were you here last week?"

Lydia taught history at Maycroft High School where Deena used to teach journalism. Unfortunately, Deena hadn't really kept up with her friends who were still teaching. Lydia looked younger than Deena remembered, her auburn hair hanging loose at her shoulders rather than pulled back in its usual low ponytail. It also looked as though she'd been coloring the gray.

"How are you?" Deena got up to give her a polite hug. "No, this is my first class. I guess it's natural to move from reporting to writing a novel. We'll see anyway."

Lydia grinned like a groupie at a Stones concert. "I'm just excited to get to be around Max Dekker. He's one of my favorite authors. I've read every one of his books."

Deena glanced over Lydia's shoulder as a handsome older man walked by. "Look," she whispered. "There he is."

Max Dekker strolled to the front of the room and set his briefcase on the desk. He looked as one would imagine a successful mystery author to look. His light-blue shirt and brown tweed jacket with suede elbow patches complimented his ruddy complexion. His salt-and-pepper hair was heavy on the salt and needed trimming. He was shorter than Deena had expected but had a nice build. His fashionista wife must have made him keep in shape.

Betty walked up and set her notepad next to Deena on the table as Lydia hurried to take her seat. "Let's go up there before he gets started," Betty said to Deena. "I'll introduce you. I brought this book for him to sign. Who knows, it might be worth something someday."

More than a little self-conscious, Deena could see all eyes were on her as she followed Betty to the desk where Max stood taking books and folders out of his old-fashioned "Death of a Salesman" style briefcase.

He narrowed his eyes as they approached. He looked at the book in Betty's hand, and he gave her a faint smile. "I see you have a copy of *Crimson Waters*. First edition. I suppose you want me to sign it."

"Of course," Betty said stiffly. She laid the book open on the desk and shot out her hand with a ballpoint pen ready and waiting.

Taking it, he said, "And your name is..."

"Betty. Betty Donaldson."

He signed the book and set the pen on the open page.

She folded up the book with the pen inside. A souvenir, of sorts. Like a foul ball caught at a ball game.

"And what did you think of it?" he asked. His face seemed poised as though waiting for a gush of praise.

"The plot was brilliant. But I didn't like the title. It didn't fit the story."

He tilted his head and narrowed his eyes.

Betty's face turned pinkish gray and she stepped to the side.

Oh, my, Deena thought. If that was her idea of flirting, she had a lot to learn.

"This is Deena Sharpe," Betty said, pushing Deena a step forward. "She's just starting tonight."

Max nodded at her and asked, "So what makes you think you can write a mystery novel, Deena Sharpe?"

Her smile fell as she stammered, "I...wrote...write...I taught journalism."

He snorted. "Ah. Another journalist thinking they can write that big, blockbuster novel." He picked up his books and walked toward the podium.

Deena crossed her arms. Had she been a cat, her back would have arched. "I don't just think it; I *know* I can write a novel. Whether or not it is a blockbuster is another thing, obviously."

"Obviously."

Betty smirked and started toward the back of the room.

Deena wasn't finished. "I would imagine the pressure, in this case, is on you. You are the one teaching us, after all."

Removing his reading glasses, Max's eyes pierced hers. "You can lead a horse to water..."

"I'm not a horse, Mr. Dekker." She turned on her heels to leave.

"Ms. Sharpe—"

"Mrs.," she said curtly, looking back over her shoulder.

"Mrs. Sharpe. I like your spunk. I'm expecting good things from you. Don't let me down."

"I won't." She turned again and marched back to her seat, her palms sweating and her heart racing.

* * *

THE NEXT HOUR ZOOMED by as Deena filled page after page of her spiral with notes. Max Dekker seemed in his element as wise teacher to the class's twenty-one students.

Deena even got up the nerve to ask a few questions, and she was glad when he nodded his head as though pleased with her participation.

Lydia raised her hand. "Mr. Dekker. It's eight o'clock. Time for our break."

"Yes. Thank you for the reminder," he said and put the cap back on his fountain pen.

"I brought homemade cookies to go with the iced tea and coffee," Lydia added, and a collective "yum" sounded throughout the room.

"Good," Betty said and headed out of the reading room.

Like a herd of heifers, the would-be authors quickly stampeded toward the break room.

Deena took her place near the back of the line. So Lydia was also a baker. Maybe she was familiar with the elusive mother-in-law dessert. She picked up a plastic cup of sweet tea and took a bite of an oatmeal raisin cookie. "This is delicious," she said to Lydia. "What's your secret?"

"I add cinnamon and pecans for extra flavor and crunch." Lydia beamed as everyone raved about her baking prowess. "You know, I've been thinking of writing a cookbook. After listening to Max Dekker these past two weeks, I think it would be a lot easier than writing a novel."

Betty walked by holding a small stack of cookies and napkins.

She must be really hungry. Deena opened her mouth to say something when a commotion near the doorway pulled her attention.

Several people filed out of the break room as Nancy frantically waved her arms, reminding everyone that "no food or drinks are allowed in the main area of the library."

Before Deena could get to the action, the word "police" drifted through the crowd back to where she stood craning to see what was happening.

Sure enough, two police officers were talking to Max Dekker. His face was stoic as he listened and nodded his head in response. After a few minutes, the officers walked away and waited near the library's main door.

Max motioned for everyone to return to their seats.

Deena brushed crumbs off the front of her blouse while Betty stood next to the wall wringing her hands. The anticipation was as thick as concrete.

Max leaned one arm on the podium and cleared his throat. "I must apologize, but it seems we will have to cut class a little short tonight. There's been an accident."

A gasp rose from the room.

"My wife, Alexis, has been killed in a car accident. The police suspect foul play."

Most everyone in the room put their hands to their mouths or chests and shook their heads in disbelief.

Deena's mouth fell open as she listened. *Is this real? Is it a hoax?* Perhaps Max Dekker was setting them up for a lesson in mystery writing 101. If so, it was just sick.

"Now, if you all will excuse me, I must tend to business." He pulled out a handkerchief and wiped his nose quickly before returning it to his pocket.

Everyone waited in stunned silence as he packed his briefcase. He glanced at the stack of cookies on the desk and put them inside along with his books and folders. He squinted his eye, focusing on the inside of the case before quickly shutting it closed.

As he clicked the metal clasps on his case, he straightened and revealed an eerily calm composure. "How ironic. It seems the mystery is about *me* this time around. I pray one of us will be able to solve it before an innocent person is blamed."

With that, he walked quickly out of the room toward the waiting officers.

For a moment, no one seemed to know what to do. Betty spread her arms and said, "I guess we'll see you all next week." It sounded more like a question than a statement.

Next week? Would he actually continue teaching their class after this?

Slowly, people rose from their chairs, gathering their things and whispering to each other.

Lydia, her face streaked with mascara-filled tears, flew up beside Deena. "That poor man. That poor, poor man." She dabbed at her eyes with a tissue.

Deena stood, her legs weak. "That was weird, right? The man finds out his wife is dead, and he doesn't miss a beat."

"He was probably in shock, don't you think?"

"I suppose. But what do you think he meant by that comment? 'Protecting an innocent person'? Was he talking about himself?"

"No! Of course not. Who would think such a talented, sensitive man would be capable of killing his wife?"

Deena tilted her head. "But he writes murder mysteries for a living."

Lydia blew her nose into her wet wad of tissues.

Trying hard not to roll her eyes, Deena picked up her satchel and led Lydia toward the exit. "Good grief. I thought the only mystery I'd have to worry about for a while would be on the pages of a book. This is one case I'm going to stay as far away from as possible."

Chapter 3

The sound of her cell phone ringing woke Deena much earlier than she would have liked. Snuggled up next to Hurley, she hesitated to answer it. Too curious to ignore it, she looked at the screen and saw it was Sandra, her best friend and the owner of the Second Chance Thrift Store.

"Why are you calling so early?" Deena asked, skipping the usual niceties.

"It's only early if you're retired and living the life of luxury. Some of us actually have to work, you know."

Deena pulled Gary's pillow behind hers and sat up. The baking book she had been reading when she fell asleep lay open on the floor. "So what's up—besides me, now?"

"Did you hear about the car wreck last night? You were in that class with Max Dekker, right?"

"Yes. The police came in during our break and told him his wife had been killed in an accident. Bless her heart. He told us they suspected foul play." Max's deadpan expression flashed before her eyes. "Do you know any more than that?"

"Ian talked to one of his friends at the sheriff's department when he was up at the jail. The guy said her brake line had been cut."

"Really? Where did the accident happen?"

"Where else? On Dead Wally's Curve."

"No way! The city really should do something about that road. It's too dark and too dangerous." Through the phone, Deena could hear the clink of a coffee cup on the table. Just the sound of Sandra knocking back fresh brew made Deena's mouth water. She sat on the edge of the bed and closed the cookbook with her feet. "Do they have any suspects?"

"Not that we know of. I was hoping you would call Dan Carson to see if he knows anything. I know he'll have a story in the paper tomorrow, but I wanted to know more today."

"Are you seriously suggesting I call him? I closed that chapter on my life." Dan Carson was the crime reporter for the *Northeast Texas Tribune* whom Deena had worked with for a short time the previous spring. "Gary would kill me if I got involved with another murder. I wouldn't blame him."

"Ah, you're no fun. At least tell me how Max Dekker reacted to the news."

"Now that was interesting," Deena said, heading toward the kitchen. "He barely reacted at all. Maybe he was in shock. He said something about making sure an innocent person wasn't accused. I wondered if he was talking about himself."

A beep sounded on Deena's phone, and she looked to see who it was. "Hey, Russell is calling. I'll stop by the store to see you later." She switched over to the other call. "Hey, what's up?"

The anxious tone of her brother's voice said more than his words. All he would tell her was to meet him at the repair shop. A flood of apprehension washed over her. Now that Russell had married Estelle, he rarely called for anything but casual conversation. She couldn't imagine what was so important he was asking her to drive the twenty miles out to Crossbow.

Of course, she agreed.

Even though Russell was a few years older, it had always fallen on her to take care of him. He suffered from PTSD and excruciating migraines. She poured coffee into the Yeti travel mug she had bought at the thrift store and threw on a pair of beige capris and a navy-blue striped shirt.

As usual, her hair was an issue. If only it were long enough for a ponytail. Worried about her brother, she smeared on some pink lip balm and skipped her less-is-more make-up routine. Luckily, her time spent by the pool had given her a rosy, bronze glow.

Hurley twirled in a circle, looking for attention.

"I promise to take you for a walk when I get home." She threw him a crunchy treat. His warm brown eyes pleaded with her to stay. "I wish I could, buddy. I'll be back soon. Cross your paws that everything will be okay."

* * *

AS SHE ROUNDED THE corner of Cricket Lane to leave her subdivision of Butterfly Gardens, Deena resisted the urge to dial up Dan on her cell phone. Although she was itching to call him, she didn't dare. When she got fired from the newspaper, she was careful not to burn bridges. Dan would be busy, and she didn't want to bug him. She'd wait and read the article in tomorrow's edition of the newspaper along with everyone else.

Her thoughts turned back to Russell. He had been doing really well since he and Estelle returned from their honeymoon in Hawaii. Deena finally felt like everything was going to be okay with him. That's why this morning's call was so unnerving. Her stomach flipped as she suppressed the urge to speculate as to why he needed to see her.

She checked her speed and slowed down her Ford Explorer. The small highway out to Crossbow wasn't the safest in the area, but it was better than the one northeast out of town headed toward the Dekker place.

When she and Gary had moved to Maycroft years ago, she heard the story of a teenager named Wally Yates who went flying around a sharp curve and lost control of his motorcycle. He crashed into a large oak tree and died on the spot. From then on, people in town referred to it as Dead Wally's Curve.

Before long, Deena spotted the sign for Cliff Abel's appliance repair shop. It was a small reputable business where Russell had worked with Cliff ever since coming back from Vietnam. Since returning from his honeymoon, Russell spent most of his time helping Estelle manage her large estate. He also spent a few days a week at the shop. Lord knows he didn't need the money. Estelle had wealth enough to buy a small country. But Russell liked working with his hands and didn't want to abandon his pre-married lifestyle.

The wooden structure that served as the repair shop needed a fresh coat of paint. A few boards were missing from the west side, and it had a definite preference for the South, based on its lean.

Russell stood outside the office drinking a beer. Sure, it was hot outside, but why was he drinking so early in the day?

Her throat tightened as she got out of the car. "So, what's up?" she asked, approaching her brother.

"It's Cliff. Come inside."

Deena followed him into the small, grubby office. The odor of oil and dirty rags assaulted her nose, making her eyes water. It was just like the early days watching her father work on his old Corvair in the garage.

Russell moved a stack of hunting magazines off a wooden chair and motioned for her to take a seat.

"You're scaring me. Tell me what happened to Cliff. Is he hurt? Is he dead?"

"Dead? For Pete's sake, no. But he is in trouble."

A tinge of relief washed over her. If he was okay, what could be so bad?

Russell stared at his half-empty bottle. "Did you hear about that accident last night on Dead Wally's Curve?"

"Yes, I was..."

"The police think Cliff may have had something to do with it."

Deena did a cartoon double take. "Cliff? What would he have to do with Alexis Dekker?"

Russell leaned on the desk and moved around some papers in front of him. "Cliff did some work for her. She has this fancy wine cooler from France that broke during their move here. Somebody gave her Cliff's name, and he agreed to try to fix it." He took a swig from the longneck bottle. "She paid him extra to pick it up from the house. It had some busted parts that Cliff had to fabricate."

Deena waved her hand at Russell, wanting him to get to the important part of the story. "And..."

"He had the dang thing fixed and ready to go three weeks ago. She kept putting him off whenever he tried to get her to come pick it up. He even offered to take it to her house, but she was too busy to be bothered."

"Was Cliff mad?"

"Not mad. More like annoyed. Finally, yesterday she told him he could bring it to the place in town where she was getting her hair done. When he got there, she didn't have the cash to pay him. Still, he loaded it in her car and left."

"I guess it was right after that when she had the accident."

"Yep. The officers said somebody cut her brake line and caused the crash. They said Cliff was the last one near her car."

Deena leaned back in her chair. "I see. So, they think Cliff was mad and tried to kill her. That seems a little drastic, don't you think?"

"Of course it does to you and me, but we're not the law."

Deena clenched her hands in her lap. "How can I help? What do you need me to do?"

"I think he needs a lawyer. He says he doesn't, but I think he does. I thought you could talk to that attorney you worked for last spring to see if he could help. I'll pay all the expenses."

A knot tied up her throat. *Here we go again.* "Where's Cliff now?"

"The officers took him in for questioning. I told him I would cover the place this afternoon." Russell swatted a fly buzzing his face. "I'm scared, Deena. You know Cliff didn't do this."

"I know. Let me call Ian and see what he says." It was handy having your best friend's husband as your lawyer and former boss.

Russell stood and plunged both hands in the pockets of his cargo shorts. His blue floral Hawaiian shirt was mis-buttoned and hanging crooked from his sagging shoulders.

Cliff and Russell were more like brothers than friends. Cliff had given Russell a job and a purpose when he came home from the Army. And Russell had been Cliff's rock after he lost his wife. That was three years ago.

Deena hadn't seen her brother this upset in a long time.

Ian answered his phone on the third ring, and she quickly explained the situation. He couldn't believe Cliff had agreed to talk to the officers without an attorney. He hung up quickly, saying he would call the Maycroft Police Department and talk to Cliff as soon as possible. Hopefully, he could get him to agree to counsel.

When she hung up, she looked at Russell.

The lines on his face softened, and he breathed easier. He rubbed his temples and sat back down in the chair.

"You're not getting a migraine, are you? Where's your medicine?"

"Maybe. I have some in my truck. I'll get it."

As he walked out to his pick-up, her chest tightened. She had been so busy going to flea markets, traveling, and attending to her antique booth, that she hadn't made much time for Russell and Estelle. She promised herself to call Estelle and set up a dinner date as soon as this mess with Cliff blew over.

Russell came back in and opened the shop's Maytag refrigerator to get a drink. He reached around several vases of cut flowers and pulled out a Dr Pepper. When he closed the door, something rattled and fell to the floor.

Deena stared at the object on the ground. "What is it?" she asked when she saw the confused look on Russell's face.

"It's...it's Cliff's pocket knife."

"So? All guys carry a pocket knife."

"I know." Russell turned back to his sister, his face ashen. "So why isn't it in his pocket?"

* * *

DEENA OFFERED TO MAKE sandwiches for lunch, leaving Russell to tend to a few customers who had stopped by to chat and check on some work Cliff was doing for them.

She and Russell ate quietly, no one mentioning the pocket-sized elephant in the room. A few minutes later, someone pulled up in the drive.

"You called a lawyer?" Cliff yelled when he came through the door. "Why would you do that?"

Russell leaned back in his chair. "For your protection. Don't worry, I'm paying for it."

Cliff pulled off his trucker hat and ran his fingers through his hair. "Man, it's not the money. It's that you think I'm guilty."

Russell stood face-to-face with Cliff. "You know I don't think that. I could never think that." His eyes drifted toward the top of the refrigerator where he had returned the pocketknife. "Murder is serious business. I didn't want you to get trapped by the cops for something you didn't do."

Cliff threw his keys on the desk. "Hey, Deena. I guess you called that attorney for me. Thanks. He seems like a good guy."

Deena nodded her head and smiled.

"You're thanking her and yelling at me? I'm the one who suggested it in the first place."

"Yeah, but she doesn't think I'm guilty of murder."

Russell pushed Cliff aside and stormed out of the office.

Cliff sat in the chair and let out a deep sigh.

Deena leaned over the desk. "You know he doesn't think you are guilty, right?"

"Yea, but I have to give him a hard time, you know."

"So how did it go?" She walked over to the refrigerator and pulled out a sandwich and a soda, being careful to shut the door gently.

"Okay, I guess." He bit into the sandwich as if it were his last meal. "They said they would get back to me."

Although his words bespoke confidence, his face told another story. He was worried.

"Is there anything I can do?" Deena asked.

Cliff took a big gulp of soda. "You can tell your nosy brother to mind his own business. Ever since he got back from his honeymoon, he's been different. I don't know if it's because of Estelle's fortune or what."

This was the first that Deena had heard of a rift between Russell and Cliff. "Really? I haven't noticed a difference. Besides, you're his best friend, and that will never change. Tell me you wouldn't do the same for him if the situation were reversed."

Cliff didn't answer. He wiped his mouth on the back of his sleeve and walked outside.

Deena waited in the office, giving the two men some time to talk. She should call Gary. She pulled her phone from her purse but stopped herself before calling him. Maybe she should tell him about Cliff in person. Then her phone rang. This time it was Ian Davis.

"I just wanted to let you know that I'm representing Cliff Abel. Obviously, I can't say anything without his permission. However, you might want to urge him to be totally forthcoming with me, if you know what I mean."

"You don't think he's being honest?" Deena couldn't imagine Cliff lying to the police.

"That's all I can say. Talk to you soon." The phone went dead.

She didn't know what to think. Was Cliff hiding something? What about that pocket knife? Russell had mentioned Cliff had been acting a little strange lately. A thought buzzed in her brain. Maybe he got mad and snapped. Deena swatted the idea from her head. No, Cliff could never kill anybody. However, she wanted to hear his version of the story. She walked outside to see the two men leaning against Russell's truck, talking like old friends.

"So is everything okay between you two?" she asked.

"Of course. Why wouldn't it be?" Russell pushed his sunglasses up on top of his head. "You women are the ones who hold a grudge."

She turned to Cliff. "I want to hear what happened yesterday. Just a short version."

Cliff looked down and kicked at the gravel.

She needed him to open up. "I don't know if Russell told you, but I'm taking a writing class with Max Dekker. We were all in the library last night when the officers came in and told him about his wife."

Cliff drew in a big breath, and then let it out slowly. "It's not much of a story really, but here goes. A few months ago, Mrs. Dekker called me up and asked if I could repair her fancy wine refrigerator. I told her I could look at it but that I had never worked on one before. She had me come out to the house to pick it up." He adjusted his cap and wiped sweat from his forehead. "It obviously had a bad motor. Thought I could fix it. A couple weeks ago, I called her and told her I had it working good as new. She told me that she and the mister would drive out here to pick it up. That's when the trouble started."

He crossed his arms. "She would call and say she would be here at a certain time, and I'd wait around, and then she'd no-show. This happened at least four times. Finally, I told her I would bring it to the house. That's when she said I should drop it off at the beauty shop on Monday. She said she'd have a check ready to pay me."

"Monday?" Deena was surprised. "Salons aren't open on Monday."

"Well, this one was. She looked to be the only customer. Anyway, when I got to the shop, she said she only had a credit card." He shook his head. "What do I look like, a bank? I was tired of messing with it, so I told her I would put it in the car, and she could mail me a check. She drives one of those small foreign jobs that has a piss ant-size trunk. I had to put the seats down to fit the dang thing in. I thought for sure I was going to rip the leather interior. That's when a guy pulled up and offered to give me a hand. We got the thing loaded in the car and both left. That was it."

Her eyes widened. "Do you know who that guy was? He sounds like the perfect alibi."

"You sound just like the cops," Cliff said and spat on the ground. "No, I don't know him. Never seen the guy before."

"What time was it when you left the shop?" As the words left her mouth, she recognized the reporter-turned-investigator tone.

"I don't know. Maybe around six thirty or six forty-five."

She switched to a softer approach. "I guess you went back home after that."

"No. I went to the cemetery. Put flowers on Gail's grave. I try to do that whenever I'm in town."

That explained all the flowers in the refrigerator. "Is that it? Is there anything else?"

"Like, did I cut the woman's brake line before I left? Is that what you're asking?"

"Of course not. You don't think I—"

"I'm sorry," Cliff said. "I know you're trying to help. It's just been a long day."

Russell patted his friend on the back. "Let's get out of this heat. A couple of beers will cool us off. I'll hang around, and we can watch the Rangers tonight just like old times. What do you say?"

"Sounds good." Cliff looked back at Deena. "Thanks for coming out. And thanks for calling Ian Davis." He lowered his head and shuffled back into the office.

"So what do you think?" Deena asked Russell when Cliff was out of earshot.

"Think about what?"

"About his story."

"Sis, I know you like to play amateur detective, but this is Cliff we're talking about, not some psycho killer."

She lowered her voice. "Russell, I can't believe you are being so naïve. You've read every conspiracy theory ever written. A murder investigation is not always about finding the truth. Sometimes the lack of evidence says more than the evidence itself. Cliff may think he has a solid alibi, but the police are going to want proof."

Russell shook his head and walked over to open the front door of her SUV. "Thank you for your help today, but we can take it from here."

She got in like an obedient child. "I need my purse from the office."

Russell headed back to retrieve it for her.

She was well aware of the importance of means, motive, and opportunity. So, if Cliff didn't do it, who did? That was the question they needed to focus on if she and Russell really wanted to help Cliff. She decided to give Russell a little time to wrap his head around the events of the day. However, she had a sneaking feeling they would soon be taking more action to help clear their friend's name.

Chapter 4

Men could be so exasperating, and Gary was no exception. Deena had shared her juicy, tragic news about Alexis Dekker and Max's reaction on Monday night, only to have Gary just shake his head and go back to watching the game. Didn't he think it was unusual that Max remained so matter-of-fact? What about that comment about foul play and guilt?

Tonight, he was just as ho-hum about Cliff having been questioned by the police. Sometimes, she thought Gary tried to remain extra nonchalant as a counterbalance to her enthusiasm. If only he knew how much it riled her.

After supper, she gave up trying to suck him into speculation on the intrigue and got ready to curl up with her Kindle. Her cell phone rang just as she was wiping face moisturizer off her hands. It was something she had ordered off the TV that was supposed to decrease the fine lines and wrinkles that were creeping around her eyes. Gary had said she seemed to be squinting more lately.

"That was Betty," Deena said as she ended the phone call. "She asked me to go with her tomorrow to take food to Max Dekker."

Gary muted the TV and gave her a sideways look. "Are you?"

"She said all I had to bring was a loaf of French bread. That should be easy enough."

Taking food in times of sickness and death was a tradition in many small communities. In the South, it was practically a religion. Plus, she was curious to see inside the house of the local celebrity. Maybe she could even get him to open up about who he thought might have wanted to harm his wife.

"Are you doing this because of Cliff or just to torture me?" Gary asked.

Deena sat on Gary's lap and put her arms around his shoulders. "Now hon, you know I wouldn't do anything to hurt you...on purpose. And yes, I'm doing this to help Cliff—and Russell, of course." She pushed his thick hair away from his face. "I want to see if Max Dekker knows any possible suspects in his wife's murder. Maybe the grief-stricken widower will respond to our sympathetic faces."

"You said you'd only be writing a mystery, not—"

Deena leaped up, causing Hurley to bark at the sudden explosion of movement. "I agree! This could be the plot for my first novel. Consider what I'm doing as research."

Gary closed his recliner into a sitting position.

Deena waited for the lecture.

His face had lost its usual playful smile. "No fun and games this time. I'm serious. There's a murderer out there, and I don't want you getting mixed up in this. Let the police do their jobs, and I'm sure Cliff will be cleared."

"Just like they cleared you and me last spring in the Wilde case?"

"Yes. Exactly like that."

Deena tensed and put her hands on her hips. "Have you forgotten that they didn't do that until Dan and I uncovered the real suspects?"

"Deena Jo, you're a stubborn woman. I'm about to turn sixty, and you are aging me more and more by the minute."

She dropped her hands and grinned. "Luckily, we have good life insurance."

Gary opened his mouth to speak, but Deena interrupted.

"By the way, did you call your mother? Did she say what day they were coming?"

"Oh, about that." Gary rubbed his hands together like a doctor announcing a devastating diagnosis. "Turns out, she's decided to come a few days earlier than the rest of the family."

"What? Did you tell her not to?" Deena stumbled backward and flopped down on the sofa.

"You know I couldn't do that. But the good news is that she can make my birthday cake. You're off the hook."

The words caught in her throat. "Are—are—you kidding me? I'm making that dessert, and it's going to be knock-your-socks-off, blue ribbon, county fair-worthy!"

"It's up to you. I know how you stress over family gatherings."

She leaned back on the sofa, covering her face with both hands. She pictured the showdown at the O.K. Corral. Her mother-in-law on one side pointing a spatula, and she on the other side brandishing a candy thermometer.

This was one shoot-out she was determined to win. She stood and stared straight at her husband who had gone back to watching the baseball game. "If you talk to your mother again, give her a message from me: I will be making your birthday cake if it's the last thing I do."

"Bite your tongue," Gary said with a sly grin. "If you get mixed up in this murder investigation, that might actually come true."

Chapter 5

Deena removed her sunglasses and adjusted her eyes to the indoor light of the library.

Lydia stood by the front desk talking to Nancy with a heaping plate of cookies.

"Those for Max Dekker?" Deena asked as she walked up to the desk.

"You mean Maycroft's newest bachelor?" Nancy cut her eyes toward Lydia.

"Oh, now..." Lydia's face flushed to a pale pink. She had on a floral dress and peekaboo pumps. She'd probably spent hours in front of the mirror.

"Didn't you have to work at school today?" Deena asked.

Lydia seemed uncomfortable with the question. "I took a personal business day. All work and no play..." She smiled and turned her attention back to Nancy.

Deena remembered hearing that Lydia had gotten divorced the previous year. That explained her overzealous interest in Max Dekker. For someone who taught history, she sure was interested in the future.

Betty walked out of the office area. "Oh good, you're here. Let me get my things and we can go." She had on her librarian pantsuit, à la Hillary Clinton.

Deena felt a bit underdressed in her navy-blue capri pants and nautical print top. "We can take my car," she offered, as the three women headed to the parking lot.

"Road trip! Isn't this fun?" Lydia was acting more like a schoolgirl than a sixty-year-old woman on the verge of retirement.

Betty, who was riding shotgun, turned to the back seat. "It's only about fifteen miles. Not much of a road trip."

Deena glanced in the rearview mirror. Lydia sat back, an excited grin on her face.

"It's creepy to think this is the same route Alexis Dekker took that night she was killed." Goosebumps formed on Deena's arms as they got closer to Dead Wally's Curve.

"Just make sure you go slow and that your brakes work," Betty said.

"Brakes? What do you mean?" Lydia asked.

"Didn't you read the article in this morning's paper?" Betty asked. "It said someone had cut her brake line. That's why she crashed. I heard they've already got a suspect. I can't wait to find out who it is. My guess is that Max Dekker did it himself."

"If you think Max is a killer, why are you taking him a casserole?" Deena asked.

"Because..." Betty clenched the side of the door and braced herself. "Slow down. Here it comes."

As Deena slowly took the curve, she saw fresh breaks in the trees and some debris on the ground. It was a morbid scene.

Deena could only imagine how upsetting it would be for Max to drive by there every time he came to town.

Lydia navigated from the back seat, telling Deena which roads to take until they reached the turnoff for the Dekker property. The smell of sweet pine trees lining the dirt road made Deena long to move to the country. However, she knew her place was in the suburbs. She liked the streetlights and sidewalks more than rattlesnakes and coyotes.

They made the last turn in the road and pulled up to an area for parking on the side of the house. When they got out of the car, Betty and Lydia stood frozen, dishes in hand. They seemed to be waiting for Deena to take the lead. Reluctantly, she led the way toward the front door carrying the loaf of bread wrapped in foil.

A large bay window with opened curtains adorned the front of the house. Deena saw the lovebirds first. Max and another woman stood on the other side of the glass, locked in a kiss one usually only saw behind closed doors. Her jaw dropped at the same time that Lydia dropped her plate of cookies. At first, she thought Lydia might have thrown it. Deena stood frozen, as though that made her invisible.

Betty turned on her heels and headed back to the car, casserole in hand.

Lydia sprinted behind her just as the merry couple turned to look out the window.

Deena finally got her sea legs and ran back to the car, got in, and peeled down the road away from the house.

Once she was back to the main road, she finally took a breath. No one said a word. She wondered if they were all thinking the same thing. Max Dekker murdered his wife to be with that other woman. If that were the case, they may have just uncovered a motive. Worse still, she knew he had seen her before she ran off.

Her mind raced with the implication of what had just happened.

"Slow down!" Betty yelled as they approached the dangerous curve.

Deena hit her brakes and squealed around the curve. She squinted her eyes and shook her head, trying to focus on the road ahead. "Sorry," she offered weakly.

"That snake," Lydia seethed from the back seat. "He's only been single two days and already has another girlfriend!"

That remark seemed ironic coming from the woman who was obviously trying to woo the man at his most vulnerable point. Maybe Lydia hadn't seen him as a suspect in his wife's murder at all.

Deena glanced sideways at Betty. Her jaw was set and her eyes glared at the road. If they were right about Max being the killer, they could all be in danger. If they were wrong, they just looked like the biggest idiots in town.

* * *

BETTY LEAPED OUT OF the car and went back inside the library almost before they came to a complete stop.

"Wait," Deena said as Lydia was about to get out of the car. "Don't you think we should talk about what just happened?"

"What's there to talk about?" Lydia asked. "That ridiculous excuse for a man is no more grieving than a cowboy winning the rodeo. All this time he had another woman on the side.

He's a heartless, careless creep in my book, and I hope I never have to see him again!" She reached for the door handle again.

"Wait," Deena repeated. "That's just the point. He *does* have another woman on the side. That means he might have a motive for murder."

"Of course, he has a motive. That seems fairly obvious."

"I think we should tell the police what we saw."

"The police?" Lydia frowned. "I'm not going to the police."

"But this could be important. Maybe Max and that woman killed Alexis so they could be together. We should head to the police department right now."

"I can't. I've got to get back home." She picked up her purse from the floorboard. "You go. Tell them everything we saw. Call me later and tell me what they said." With that, she got out of the car.

"Bye..." Deena said to the closed car door. *How do I get myself into these messes?*

She needed to think things through before going to the police. Her plan had been to work on her booth after the visit to Max's house. She drove toward the antique mall, her mind still reeling. Several cars were parked out front. Probably tourists or other sellers working on their booths.

Facing the owner, Janet, or anyone else she knew right now felt impossible. She had too much on her mind and needed to unload it. Maybe she would go to the thrift shop and talk to Sandra.

Her thoughts turned to Cliff. Could this be the break he needed to get the cops off his back? She had an idea. She drove several more blocks to Ian Davis's law office. If anyone would know what to do, Sandra's husband would.

Chapter 6

This was the first time she'd been back there since the Wilde case last spring. From the outside, Ian Davis' office looked the same as when she had worked for him a whole week as an investigator. The job had been brief but eventful. A tarp on the roof next to the brick chimney actually made the old Victorian house look more dilapidated than ever.

Deena opened the door and was pleased to see that renovations had taken place on the inside. Walls housed proper offices and the whole place had a fresh coat of paint. The mildew smell and the "Keep Out" sign in front of the staircase were gone.

"Deena Sharpe. How are you?" Rob stood and welcomed her into the newly created waiting area.

"Nice to see you," she said and shook his hand. "So, you're still here."

"Yep. My internship ends in December, and then I'm moving to St. Louis. I suppose you want to see Ian about the Dekker case. I'll let him know you're here."

Being too nosy for her own good, she glanced at the papers and files on Rob's desk. Nothing about Cliff or Max caught her eye.

Rob came around the corner. "Head on back. His office is the last one on the left."

She passed two offices and what appeared to be the copy room. Ian's door was open. "Hey, boss," she joked as she stuck her head inside.

"Have a seat," Ian said, in his I'm-all-business manner. "I'm glad you're here. I need your help."

Deena took a step backward. Not again. "I was just kidding about the boss thing."

"It's not that." He motioned to the chair across from his desk.

As usual, his light brown hair needed a trim, making him look even more boyish than he already did.

She sat down slowly. "I like what you've done with the place. Looks really professional."

"Thanks. We got some money from the state to do renovations. Anyway, I talked to Cliff this morning, and he gave me permission to speak to you and your brother about his case."

"Okay..."

"Seems like Detective Guttman isn't completely buying his story."

"Who is Detective Guttman? Is he new?"

"Don't you read the newspaper anymore?"

She shot him a sheepish grin. "I get all my news from the grapevine these days."

Ian rolled his eyes. "Linus Guttman is the county judge's nephew. No nepotism there, I'm sure." Ian tapped his pen repeatedly on the desk. "He thinks he's a hot-shot because he came here from Philadelphia. Word is that they ran him off."

"Ugh. Just what we need in sleepy, old Maycroft."

"Seems like he's using this case to try to make a name for himself. Doesn't understand the people around here. He assumes everyone is rotten to the core."

Deena leaned forward. "That's why I'm here. I think I have another suspect *and* a motive."

Ian lifted an eyebrow. "Shoot."

"Max Dekker."

"The husband is always a suspect. Motive?"

She told him about the hospitality visit and what they had seen through the window.

Ian jotted down some notes. "Do you have any idea who this woman was? What did she look like? Did you see anyone else there? Any strange cars?"

Before he could go on, she held up both hands. "Hold your horses, counselor. One question at a time. No, I didn't recognize her. She was short, probably about five-foot-four, and had light-colored hair. It was either blonde or gray. I didn't get a good look at her face. I only saw her and Max in front of the window. As for cars, it was my first time out there. I know I saw at least one car, but I really don't remember it."

"Give me the names of the two other women who were with you."

"Do I have to?" She frowned and shifted in her chair.

"What's the problem?"

"I've gotten a little used to this murder investigation stuff, but my friends haven't. What if Max or his gal pal comes after us?" She folded her arms across her chest. "I don't need more enemies."

"You said that Dekker saw all of you, right?"

"I know he saw me. I'm not sure about the others."

"Okay, then. Let me talk to Detective Gutt-*less* and tell him what you told me. He won't do anything to put you in danger. He knows he has to check out every lead before he makes an arrest if he wants the conviction to stick."

"Arrest? You mean Cliff?"

"That's the way he's leaning."

"What can I do to help?"

Ian pulled a clean sheet of paper out of his legal pad. "This is the make and model of the car driven by the man Cliff says helped him load the cooler into Mrs. Dekker's car. Get Cliff to give you a full description of him. You and Russell check all the businesses in that shopping area to see if anyone knows him. That guy's his best alibi." He handed the paper to Deena. "We'd do it ourselves, but Amy left a few weeks ago, and I haven't found a good replacement."

"This sounds easy enough. Nothing dangerous. Anything else?"

"Just one more thing. Cliff's timeline. It doesn't add up. There's a gap of time between him being at the salon and the cemetery. See what you can get out of him."

"Will do." She stood to leave. A queasy feeling swirled in Deena's stomach. She was getting in too deep again. "And thanks, Ian. I owe you one."

"Hardly. I'm the one who owes you. But who's keeping score."

Her phone rang, but she didn't recognize the number. It was Detective Guttman. He said he needed her to come down to the police station to answer a few questions. She agreed and hung up.

"You see? News travels fast in this town. One of my friends must have called him about our visit. He probably wants to get my version to corroborate the information."

Ian shook his head. "Call me after the interview. Remember, stick to the facts."

She nodded her head. "Tell Sandra I'll get by to see her soon."

As she walked out to the parking lot, tires squealed from the far side of the building, causing her to jump. She turned quickly, but the car or truck was already gone. Already a little jittery, she tried to tell herself it was nothing. At least she hoped it wasn't.

* * *

SITTING IN THE INTERVIEW room where she and Ian had talked to their client last spring gave Deena a weird sense of déjà vu. Hopefully, this would go quickly, and she could go to the antique mall to work on her booth. Obviously, Lydia must have changed her mind and called the police. All she needed to do here was corroborate what Lydia told the detective. Her stomach growled reminding her she'd skipped lunch.

The door opened, and in strolled the detective. His crumpled blue suit appeared a size too large. It reminded her of some of the high school boys who would wear their father's suit under their graduation gowns. At least they had the sense to wear dress shoes. The detective's white Nikes drew her eyes to the ground as he approached.

"Detective Guttman." He sat down without reaching out his hand as was customary in these parts.

Deena reached across the table and introduced herself.

Guttman hesitated before reluctantly returning the gesture. He immediately wiped his hand on his pants leg.

Either a chauvinist or a germaphobe, Deena surmised. How could either get this far in law enforcement? This boy was going to have to learn some manners if he planned on making it here in the South.

"I have a few questions for you." He pulled a small pad of paper and a pen from his shirt pocket.

"You're welcome," Deena said, with her warmest fake smile.

"What?"

"Oh, I thought you were going to say, 'Thank you for coming down here.' That's what Detective Evans would have said."

"Captain Evans."

"Really? I must congratulate him on the promotion. Such a polite man. Good manners, don't you think?"

"Whatever. Where were you this morning at around eleven o'clock?"

"Well, as I'm sure you know, I was at Max Dekker's house. That shouldn't be a surprise. I'm sure Lydia told you the same thing."

"Who's Lydia?"

So this is how we're going to play the game. He's going to be cagey like he's some kind of super sleuth. Her muscles tightened, and she clenched her jaw.

"Lydia Ivey."

"Who's she?"

"History teacher at the high school."

"And why do you assume I talked to her?"

Deena rolled her eyes. "Because she called you, of course. She had to be the one who told you we went to Max Dekker's house. I told her I was going to contact the police, but she obviously called you and told you what we did."

"I see." The detective scribbled on the notepad. "And by 'we' you mean..."

"Myself, Lydia Ivey, and Betty Donaldson. She *did* tell you about Betty, right?"

"And what were you—the three of you—doing at Max Dekker's house?"

"We were there to offer our condolences and to bring him a meal. That's what we do here in the South. We are polite and offer comfort to people in need."

"And Mr. Dekker was in need because..."

Deena crossed her arms, her patience wearing thin. "Because he just lost his wife."

"Uh-huh." More scribbling. "And what is your relationship to Mr. Dekker?"

"I have no relationship with him. I just met him two days ago. He's teaching a class at—"

"And why weren't you in class the first week? It is my understanding you just started on Monday. The day Mrs. Dekker was killed."

Deena's jaw dropped. "Detective Guttman. Why is that pertinent to what we saw at Max Dekker's house?"

He loosened his tie. "I'll ask the questions, Mrs. Sharpe."

Heat rose from her neck as she tried to keep her anger in check. "I came here to make a statement and to tell you what we saw at the Dekker house."

"And what did you see?" He tilted his head as though questioning a child.

"*We* saw Max Dekker kissing a woman. On the lips. Two days after his wife was murdered."

Guttman's eyebrow lifted above his beady dark eyes. "And how did you manage to see this? Were you inside the house? Were you spying on him?"

"Heavens, no! Like I said, we were there to bring food. He and that woman were standing by the window in the front room. Don't you think that sounds suspicious?"

"What did you do when you witnessed this alleged kiss?"

"Lydia dropped her cookies."

"Dropped her cookies? Is that some expression you Southerners use?"

"No. She had a plate of cookies and dropped them on the ground. Then we all ran back to the car and left."

"Why?"

"We didn't want him to see us, of course. Although, I think he did."

"You think he saw *you* or you and your alleged companions?"

Deena pursed her lips. "I'm not sure." She stood to leave. "Look, you have my statement. It clearly proves Max Dekker had another woman on the side and a motive for murdering his wife. You should be investigating him instead of Cliff Abel."

The detective got out of his chair and took a step toward her. "You know Cliff Abel?"

His glare sent a shiver down her spine. She resisted the urge to back away. "Yes. He's a friend. My brother works with him."

The detective stood nearly a foot taller. She raised her chin and returned his stare.

"Mrs. Sharpe, I'm advising you not to leave town."

"What? Me?" She felt like she'd just been kicked by a mule. Apparently, she'd gone from witness to suspect faster than a New York minute. "This is all a big misunderstanding," she said, softening her tone.

Deena thought about her accomplices. Who knows what Lydia might have told him. Maybe she was more unstable than Deena realized. She knew she could count on Betty to be factual and to the point. "Just talk to Betty Donaldson at the library. She'll back up everything I told you."

The detective eyed her as if taking a mental photograph. "I'm sure she will."

Chapter 7

The ingredients mocked her. Sugar, eggs, corn syrup, vanilla, and pecans. The clean, new candy thermometer looked like a spear ready to pierce her heart. Who would put candy in cake anyway?

Gary's mother, that's who. Deena stared at the notecard with the hand-written recipe. She squinted to focus. Lately, she had noticed it was more difficult to read small print than she wanted to admit. She picked up the card and moved it closer and farther from her eyes. Making it easier to see wasn't going to make it any easier to prepare.

"Chocolate swirl divinity cake," she said aloud to Hurley, who sat ready to be her taste tester.

Gary loved divinity. It was one of the few sweets he liked. He preferred most of his desserts on the savory side. Deena, on the other hand, was a card-carrying member of Chocoholics Anonymous.

Early in their married life, she had attempted to make her husband the fluffy Southern delicacy. Bless his heart, he always tried to eat it and not let on that most of it ended up in the dumpster at work. Her last attempt at trying to prepare it came out so wrong that she ripped up the linoleum countertop trying to scrape off the blobs that had stuck there. They had to pay to have them replaced. That was in their old house. Now she had granite counter tops, and so far, they'd proven indestructible. However, she had even less confidence now.

This was a test run of divinity. It was Friday morning, and Gary's birthday party was still a week away. "If I can master the divinity, the rest should be a piece of cake." She looked down at Hurley who obviously didn't appreciate her pun.

Step one of the recipe card simply read, "Make a batch of pecan divinity"—as though it were that simple. Deena decided not to take any chances. She had turned to Pinterest and found Paula Deen's recipe. How could she go wrong?

Deena wished her mother, an average cook for the time, had made her spend more time helping in the kitchen instead of letting her stay in her room reading. Maybe she wouldn't struggle as much as she did when it came to pots and pans.

She had just enough time to attempt this batch before picking up Russell to go in search of Cliff's mystery eyewitness. After she botched her interview at the police station, Ian had assured her he would smooth things over with Detective Guttman.

She measured out four cups of sugar with the precision of a chemist and added them to the large saucepan. Next, she added a cup of cold water and a cup of light corn syrup. She turned on the burner and began stirring.

So far, so good. She had already separated the egg whites and had them ready in a large bowl. She knew she was at a disadvantage only having a hand mixer and not a bowl mixer. She beat the egg whites. She needed them to form stiff peaks. But how stiff was stiff? She gave them a few extra beats, just in case.

Then she remembered the candy thermometer. She put it in and clipped it to the side of the saucepan. The temperature soared. Just then, the telephone rang. It was the landline phone in the bedroom. No way was she going to drop everything just to answer the phone.

But what if it was Gary or Russell? Maybe something was wrong. No, it was probably just a sales call. After all, anyone who knew her would call her cell phone. The ringing stopped, and she relaxed.

Why don't they make a digital candy thermometer with numbers a person could actually see? She leaned in close to the boiling mixture trying to focus on the tiny numbers, looking for 255 degrees.

Then her cell phone rang. Uh-oh. She had set it on the dining room table, safely out of harm's way. Maybe something really was wrong. If she just turned the temperature on the stove down a little, it shouldn't hurt anything. The phone was like a screaming baby. It seemed to ring louder, urging her to come tend to its needs.

She turned the knob on the stove and rushed to grab her cell phone. It was Russell. "What do you want?" she asked.

"Whoa, Nelly. What's eating you?"

"Divinity. Is something wrong? Did you just call my other phone?"

"Yeah. I didn't have on my reading glasses and must have hit the other number."

"Ugh." She looked across the open bar at the steam pouring out of the pot. "I'm in the middle of something."

She rushed back to the stove. The smell of burnt sugar filled the air before she even looked inside to see the scorched bottom of the pot. She looked at the knob and realized she had turned it to a hotter temperature instead of cooler. She moved the pan off the burner just before it was about to bubble over the sides.

Her cell phone slipped, but she caught it before it slid into the hot mixture. She stared at the pan. "This better be important."

"Actually, it's not. I was just making sure you still wanted me there at ten thirty."

"Yep."

"Okay. See you then."

Great. It will me take that long to clean up this mess.

* * *

"WHAT'S ESTELLE UP TO today?" Deena asked as Russell got into her blue Ford Explorer. "I'm surprised she let you out of the chicken coop today."

"Ah. She's not that bad. She just likes having me around." Russell fastened his seatbelt. "Besides, she's having her 'spa day.'" He emphasized the phrase with air quotes.

"That's surprising. She never seemed like someone who would enjoy that sort of pampering."

"You have no idea," Russell said. "Ever since you took her to get a pedicure before our wedding, she's been going every other week it seems. She gets everything painted, plucked, filed, or waxed. And I mean *everything*!"

"Okay. TMI, big brother. I get the picture."

Russell chuckled.

She wrinkled her nose. "Not *that* picture. You know what I mean."

At ten forty-five, Deena pulled into a parking space at the Riverdale Shopping Center. "Let's start at the doc-in-the box. It's probably got the most employees."

Russell nodded. "Speaking of pictures, I forgot to show you this." He reached into the pocket of his shorts and pulled out a small stack of folded papers. "Cliff gave me a description of the guy we're looking for, and I made this drawing." He unfolded the papers and passed them to Deena. "I made a few copies."

"I had forgotten how well you draw," she said, admiring the pencil drawing. "So this is the guy we're looking for, huh?"

"Yep. I had a hard time getting the mouth right, but Cliff said it was a pretty good likeness."

"Nice work. This should really help."

They headed into the Maycroft Medi-Clinic.

A receptionist sat behind a sliding glass window.

A young woman tried to distract her busy toddler who seemed intent on slapping the front of the waiting room's aquarium.

As she and Russell approached the window, the plump, middle-aged receptionist pointed to the sign-in sheet on the counter.

Shaking her head, Deena motioned for the woman to slide open her glass window.

The woman slowly pushed back the glass. "You have to sign in and have a seat. I'll call you when it's your turn," she said curtly. She slammed the glass closed before Deena could utter a sound.

Russell stepped in front of Deena and smiled at the woman. He waved as though they were best friends.

She smiled back. Russell was usually shy, but people always responded to his friendly demeanor. Opening the glass again, she asked, "May I help you?"

"We're not here to see a doctor. We're here to see you."

Like the doorkeeper of Oz, Deena expected her to utter the words, *Well, that's a horse of a different color.*

Instead, she pushed her short locks behind her ear and asked, "What can I do ya for?" She batted her eyes through puffy lids. She apparently liked her position of power.

Deena couldn't help but think of the school secretary who everyone had suspected helped herself to kids' lunches when they were brought to school by anxious parents. Why was it that people who worked in doctors' offices often looked so unhealthy?

Russell's sweet smile seemed to melt the receptionist's defenses. "I can tell that you are obviously in charge of this place, so you can hopefully help us out. We're looking for someone who may have been here last Monday. This guy." He held out the picture.

The woman's flirty eyes quickly narrowed. "Never seen him before." Through tightened lips, she asked, "Are you private eyes or what? I already told that detective I didn't see nothin' or nobody suspicious that day."

"We're not detectives. We are—friends of—uh..."

Deena stepped forward. "We are helping out with the investigation. Would it be possible for us to speak to other staff members?"

A side door opened, and a nurse called for the mother and her son.

"No, it wouldn't be possible."

Deena took the picture from off the counter and wrote Russell's name and cell phone number across the bottom. She handed it back to Ms. Hospitality. "If you could, please show this picture to your colleagues. If anyone knows him, give us a call."

The woman snatched the picture and shut the window so hard it rattled the wall.

Deena led the way out. "What do you think? Will she help us?"

"I doubt it," Russell said. "That picture is probably in the paper shredder as we speak."

"Maybe not. I noticed a couple of Agatha Christie paperbacks next to her computer. Maybe she likes a good mystery and will keep her eyes open."

"Or maybe she is a slacker who reads on the job instead of taking care of business."

Deena stopped walking. "Since when did you get so cynical about people?"

"Since my best friend got questioned for murder."

Deena stared over at the Manely Beauty Salon and noticed it was fairly crowded for the middle of the week. "Ready to go in?"

"You know, maybe you should check out the beauty shop without me. They're probably not used to guys being in there."

"First of all, Fred Flintstone, no one says 'beauty shop' anymore. It's a *salon*. And lots of men get their hair cut in there. It's where Gary and I both go."

"Gary? Huh. Well, you're not gonna catch me in there with all that estrogen and peroxide. I go to a barber." He jutted out his chin. "Like a real man."

Deena shook her head. "Good grief. I'll go here, and you check out those other businesses. Call me when you're done."

He handed her a copy of the drawing and headed to the other end of the parking lot.

Who knew he was still living in the Stone Age. Luckily, Estelle was an old-fashioned woman, or else she probably wouldn't be able to put up with him. She likely found his chauvinism charming.

The sound of blow dryers and chatter greeted Deena inside the shop. Unfortunately, there were no men in the place. She wanted to give Russell a big "I told you so." Oh well, she had more important matters to attend to.

Her stylist, Kristy, was chatting away with a woman getting highlights. "Oh, hey," Kristy said when she spotted Deena. "I didn't see your name on the books. Do you have an appointment?"

"No, I'm here looking for someone. Or rather, someone who might know someone."

"Huh?"

Deena held up Russell's drawing. "I'm trying to find anyone who might know this guy."

Kristy set down the brush and hair dye bowl and took the picture. After studying it, she handed it back to Deena and shook her head. "Nope. Never seen him. Who is he anyway?"

Deena wasn't sure how much she should say. She trusted Kristy but didn't want to speak openly in front of the stranger in her chair. She motioned for Kristy to follow her backward a few feet. "Were you here Monday night when Alexis Dekker was here?" Deena asked in a whisper.

Kristy glanced over her shoulder at her client. "No. That was Melissa. Why? What do you know?"

Deena looked down, fumbling with the picture. "I just need to talk to her."

"Okay. I'm almost finished putting on this color. Then I need to tell you something."

Deena nodded and turned to the other side of the shop where Melissa was showering her client's head with hairspray.

How ironic that Melissa was known for creating "big hair" when she kept her own blonde locks cropped short in a boy cut. She was probably in her thirties but seemed younger. All Deena really knew about her was that she was originally from New Orleans and had moved to Maycroft to live with her aunt and uncle.

As soon as the client left, Deena walked up. "Hey, Melissa. Do you have a minute?"

"Um, not really. I have another client coming and..."

"It won't take long, I promise."

Grabbing a broom, Melissa began sweeping around her chair. "What do you want?"

"I'm trying to figure out who this guy is. Do you know him?" She held the picture out.

Melissa grabbed it, took a quick look, and shoved it back at Deena. "No. Is that all?"

"Are you sure? You didn't happen to see him here Monday night when...um...Alexis Dekker was here, did you?"

The broom clattered to the floor, and Melissa quickly bent down to retrieve it. "What are you, a cop? I already talked to that detective."

"No, no," Deena said. "I'm a friend of Cliff Abel's. I'm just trying—"

"Murderer!"

Suddenly, everything and everyone in the shop froze. Deena looked around to see all eyes on her. She looked at Kristy, imploring her to help.

Kristy grabbed her blow dryer and turned it on even though her client was still getting color applied. She waved her hand for her colleagues to carry on. A low hum returned to the shop.

Deena turned back to Melissa. "What do you mean?"

Melissa kept her distance but lowered her voice. "Cliff Abel got pissed off and cut that woman's brake line. He caused that accident. He killed her."

"You're wrong."

Melissa's nostrils flared as she studied Deena. She started to say something but stopped. She leaned the broom against the wall and walked off to the back room of the shop.

Deena could feel the intensity rise again but kept her cool. She walked over to the reception desk. "Could you do me a favor? Please ask around to see if anyone recognizes this man. There's a number on the bottom they can call."

Kristy followed Deena out the door and led her around the side of the shop away from the front windows. "After what happened last spring, I'm surprised you're investigating another murder."

Before Deena could explain, Kristy continued. "Anyway, I just wanted you to know that Melissa has been acting a little strange since this thing happened Monday."

"It's not that surprising considering one of her clients is dead."

"Yeah, except she hated Alexis Dekker."

"How do you know?"

"She complained about her all the time. Not that I blame her. For one, the woman insisted on coming in on Monday nights when the shop was closed. She must have thought she was too good to be here with the regulars. Also, she never liked the way Melissa did her hair and told her so."

"Then why did Melissa keep her as a client?"

"Because, the woman paid her a hundred dollars extra for working on Mondays. Like the rest of us, Melissa needed the extra cash."

"You don't think Melissa did something to cause the accident, do you?"

"No, of course not. But..."

"What is it?"

"Well, you saw how defensive she was. She's been acting that way all week. She won't talk to any of us. It's unnatural, ya know?"

"I suppose."

"Look, I gotta go before Mrs. Waldrop turns into Strawberry Shortcake. I just thought you should know."

Kristy scooted around the corner and left Deena to muddle over the information.

One of the reasons Deena liked Kristy was because she was cool-headed and didn't spread baseless gossip. Sure, she knew all the latest town dirt, but she didn't blab about it to her clients. She didn't seem to take delight in other people's misery as some people did.

So for her to talk about Melissa like that meant she must really be bothered. Should Deena tell Ian about it? Detective Guttman? The last thing she wanted was to take the heat off Cliff just to turn it up on another innocent person.

For now, she would keep the info to herself. Russell didn't need to know either. She trusted her brother, of course, but he seemed desperate to help his friend. She was afraid of what he might do with this new information.

Chapter 8

Deena's cell phone rang about the time she caught up to Russell who hadn't had any luck tracking down the elusive stranger either. She was surprised to see it was Gary calling.

"Hey, are you still with Russell?" he asked.

"Yep. We are over by the salon. Why?"

"I came home for lunch and something seems to be wrong with the sink. It's backing up, and the disposer just growls when I turn it on. I tried turning that crank-thingy, but nothing happened."

Deena pictured Gary wearing his dress pants, trying to get on the floor to check the garbage disposer without messing up his clothes.

"Do you think Russell would mind coming over to have a look at it?" he asked.

"I'll ask him." Deena had a suspicion of what the problem was but didn't want to get into it. "See you tonight."

Even though they were very different in their interests and their ways of doing things, in some ways, Russell and Gary were a lot alike. They'd both give you the shirt off their back, it was just that Gary would wash and iron his first. Russell liked working with his hands; Gary liked keeping his clean. Deena knew she was lucky to have both her husband and her brother around.

Deena shuddered. Maybe that was the situation with Max Dekker. He had two women in his life to serve different needs. One thing she knew for sure: The woman he was kissing was definitely *not* his sister.

* * *

"IT LOOKS LIKE SOMEONE poured glue down here," Russell said as he shined a flashlight into the sink drain.

Debating whether to tell him what she did, Deena finally decided to 'fess up. "It's not glue. Actually, it's divinity."

"You mean, like the candy?"

"Yep. I was making it this morning when you called and it overcooked so I had to throw it out but it started to harden so I turned on the disposer and then—"

Russell held up his hand. "Stop. I get it. You fried the disposer motor, so I'll have to replace it. I'll take out the broken one and go to the hardware store to buy a new one."

"You're the best," Deena said. "Would you care if I run up to the thrift store to talk to Sandra while you do that? I'll pay you back for the new one."

"No problem," he said. "I'll get my toolbox out of the trunk."

Deena tossed Hurley a treat. "Be back soon, buddy."

Hurley knew the routine. He walked over to a small rug near the fireplace, took a few turns, and plopped down to wait for her return.

Russell came back in with his tools and got right to work.

She grabbed her latest Kate Spade purse as Russell mumbled something from under the sink.

Deena rarely worried about her safety in the suburbs. Driving into her neighborhood was like being tucked into bed for a good night's sleep. Sure, Maycroft had some of the same issues as Dallas and Houston, but everything was on a much smaller scale.

As she pulled out of the driveway, Christy Ann was getting out of her car, her youngest of three children in tow. The other two must be in school. The little girl had ponytails with a bow as big as her head. It was a wonder she could keep her head upright.

Deena drove into town anxious to see her friend. Sandra was about fifteen years younger than Deena and had happily become pregnant with her first child back in the spring. Although Deena had a niece and two nephews from Gary's sister, they lived out of state, which made it harder to dote on them.

Sandra's baby would be the closest she would ever come to having a grandchild, and Deena had already made up her mind to shower the baby with love and gifts. After all, Sandra was her best friend and more like a sister at times.

She pulled up in front of the thrift shop and parked among several other cars. Deena was glad to see business booming. That meant more money to support the animal shelter.

The bells on the door jingled as Deena went inside. Sandra was behind the cash register helping a customer. At six months pregnant, she was glowing like a disco ball, sending sparkles all around the shop. She glanced up at Deena and smiled.

Deena pointed to her favorite aisle where Sandra kept the glass items and knick-knacks and headed that direction. Since she had spent most of the summer paring her backlog of inventory down from Mount Everest to Bunker Hill, it was time to hunt for more treasures for her antique booth.

An old Swiss music box caught her eye. It was like one her mother kept on the dresser when she was growing up. She and Gary were making plans to visit her parents in Hawaii for the holidays. Maybe she should buy the music box as a gift for her mother.

"Boo!"

Deena spun around to see Sandra standing behind her. "Lord have mercy! You don't need to be scaring me like that. Bladder control is one of the casualties of old age, you know."

"And of pregnancy."

Deena took a step back. "Well, I'm glad to see you are finally showing. Now both of us have a potbelly. You look great, by the way." She patted Sandra's stomach.

"Aw, shucks. Follow me." Sandra led the way to the front counter and climbed onto her stool.

Deena set the music box down and looked around for nearby customers. Not seeing any, she leaned in and whispered, "So what's the latest on Alexis Dekker's murder? Has Ian talked to the detective or the DA?"

"You know I'm not allowed to tell you confidential information." Sandra leaned in. "But they do have another suspect."

"Max Dekker, right?"

"No. It's a man from Houston. That's all I could get out of Ian."

Deena rolled her eyes. "Ugh. Your husband is so ethical. Sometimes it's annoying."

"Tell me about it," Sandra said. "He insinuated that there was probably more information online, but I haven't had time to check. Between the store, doctor's appointments, and getting the nursery ready, I haven't had time to do much of anything."

"Well, I've got nothing but time. I'll look as soon as I get home."

"I thought you were writing a novel? What happened to that idea?"

"I've only been to one class and have no idea if there will even be another."

"Maybe you can write about Mrs. Fitzhugh's murder. That would make a great story."

"Nah. Nobody would believe it. I have been tossing around a few ideas, though."

"Can I be a character in your book? *Pa-leeeese*?"

"We'll see. After all, every crime fighter needs a side-kick."

Sandra got up to unlock the dressing room for a customer.

The sight of her from the side brought a grin to Deena's face. She couldn't wait to see that baby.

"Do you know the gender yet?" Deena asked as Sandra sat back down. "You promised you would tell me as soon as you found out."

"Ian and I decided we wanted to be surprised."

Deena's mouth dropped open.

"Then we changed our minds. We will find out at my appointment next week."

Deena clapped her hands like a kid at the circus. "Yay! Auntie Deena wants to start buying clothes and toys."

"Speaking of Auntie Deena, I have a big—I mean, *really* big favor to ask."

Here it was. Sandra was going to ask her and Gary to be the baby's godparents. What would she say? Yes, of course. But that was a huge responsibility. She should probably talk it over with Gary. But Gary would agree with whatever she wanted.

"Yoo-hoo. Deena?" Sandra waved her hand in front of Deena's face.

"Oh, sorry," she said, returning from her stupor. "Yes."

"Yes what?"

"Yes to your question."

"But you don't even know what I was going to ask."

Deena smiled and tilted her head. "So ask."

Sandra cleared her throat. "I wanted to know if you would be willing to take over the store for a while when the baby is born?"

Deena felt her face drop and start to flush.

"I know it's a lot to ask, but you're the only person I trust. Plus you're retired—except for this new writing gig."

Deena blinked her eyes and then stared at her friend.

"Never mind. Sorry I asked. I can just close the shop for a few months." Sandra put her head down and fiddled with a receipt book.

"No. I mean, yes. Of course, I'll do it. I'd be glad to help."

"Really?" The shine returned to Sandra's face. She shuffled around the counter and threw her arms around Deena. "I knew I could count on you."

Deena's breathing returned to normal, although the disappointment still pinched her chest. "This means I get first choice at buying the donated goodies, right?"

"We'll see about that. You have to realize that it's not all glittery treasure that comes through here. You should have seen the greasy handkerchief I pulled out of a box of designer women clothes left outside the back door this morning."

"Designer clothes? Anything my size?"

"I haven't had a chance to go through them yet. You can sneak back there and look on the rack by the door."

Deena loved the perks of being best friends with the store-owner. Knowing Sandra, though, she would still charge her the same as any customer. Since the money went to the animal shelter, Sandra would ask top dollar for designer clothes.

Deena instantly recognized the labels on the high-end clothes. "St. John, Ann Taylor, Armani." Something stopped her. She gasped and stared at the label neatly stitched inside the dark gray suit jacket. It read: *Made exclusively for Alexis Dekker*.

* * *

SOMETHING NAGGED AT her as she drove home. Why would Max Dekker have already gotten rid of his wife's clothes? If he were guilty of murder, that would look awfully suspicious. Did he think no one would recognize them? For a man who wrote murder mysteries, that would seem like a totally amateur move. And what about the greasy handkerchief? Who would stick that in there with all those gorgeous suits and dresses?

Something didn't add up. As soon as she could, she would go online and see what she could find out about this suspect from Houston. She was surprised that Russell's car was gone when she pulled back into the garage. That was quick, even with his experience fixing things.

As she sat in the car, she made a decision. She texted Sandra. "Tell Ian about getting Alexis's clothes at the thrift store." Ian might think nothing of it, or he might act on it. Either way, it was one less thing for Deena to wonder about.

The phone in the bedroom was ringing when she walked into the house. She charged that direction, nearly tripping over Hurley. It stopped ringing before she could get to it. She sat on the bed catching her breath. It was time to start exercising again, that was for certain, especially if she were going to go back to work. Had she really agreed to mind the store for Sandra when the baby came? What was she thinking? Retirement life had made her fat and happy.

Her cell phone rang this time. "Russell? Did you just call my home phone?"

"Yes. You didn't answer."

"Stop doing that. Always call my cell."

"So why do you still bother having a land-line?"

"I use it to call my cell phone when I can't find it."

"Whatever. I called to tell you I haven't replaced the disposer yet. I went to the hardware store. They were *way* overcharging for them. I'll get one from Cliff at wholesale and install it in the morning."

"Sounds good. Gives me an excuse to go out to dinner."

"Oh, I forgot something. I turned off your water at the street. The shut-off valve under the sink was broken. I'll replace that in the morning, too. Don't turn it back on or you'll flood the kitchen."

"So does that mean we have no water?"

"Yeah, but it's only for one night. Pretend you're a pioneer. It'll be fine."

Deena wasn't so sure. Immediately, a desert formed in her throat. Hopefully, there was still iced tea in the fridge. She got a pack of bottled water from the garage and put it in the refrigerator to chill. That should do it. Her worry finally subsided.

Ice cubes tinkled in the glass as she sat down at the desk in her office. It had been a while since she had researched anything other than the prices of her newly found treasures. She put in Max Dekker's name and up came hundreds of listings involving his various mystery novels. Obviously, she wasn't going to wade through all that.

Wikipedia, the nemesis of every high school teacher, had always been her best friend when doing her own research (although she would never have admitted it to her students). She found the profile on Max and read it closely.

The details of his early life were unremarkable. He was born in El Paso and had attended the University of Texas where he taught creative writing before hitting it big with his first novel. He moved to Manhattan and married his literary agent, Alexis Jamison. They divorced after eighteen years of marriage.

He later married a woman named Barbara Conroy. The article contained no specific details about this second wife. Deena scrolled back to the top to see if it listed any children for Max Dekker. There were none. She continued reading where she had left off.

After just two years with his second wife, he divorced her and re-married Alexis. *And they say women are fickle.* He must have had some sort of mid-life crisis. Probably thought the grass was greener on the other side of the fence. *Men.*

Deena thought about Gary and his impending birthday. She had anticipated he might go through some sort of crisis at fifty, but it didn't happen. At fifty-five, nothing. Here he was about to turn sixty. The clock was ticking. But this was Gary. Calm, rational Gary. Surely, he would remain the same man she married all those years ago.

She turned her attention back to the Dekkers. Nowhere in the article did it mention Houston. She decided to add it to Google as a search term. Listings for his best-seller *Bounty Beyond the Border* came up. She quickly scanned the first article. The book was set in Houston.

Ugh. That was no help. She scrolled through and found other stories, book signings, and speaking engagements in Houston.

The low hum of the garage door opening signaled Gary's arrival. He came through the door, and she looked up just in time to see him zoom past the office door and shout, "Hi, hon" on his way to the bedroom. She instantly knew what that meant. Nothing newsworthy there.

Duh, she thought and slapped her forehead. She was looking for something *news worthy*. She added "Houston Chronicle" as a search term. There among the book reviews, a headline that attracted her attention—"Copycat Murder Mirrors Best-selling Novel."

She opened the article and waited for it to load. Could this be it? She read the brief news story. It detailed a crime where a woman was murdered by gang member initiates in the same way Max Dekker had described a killing in his Houston-based novel. The victim's husband was quoted as blaming Dekker for giving them the idea. The police detective who investigated the crime said it was highly unlikely that the wanna-be gang members were "avid readers," and it was likely just a coincidence. The article stated that there was no comment given by the author.

"Deena," Gary shouted from the back of the house.

She recognized that as her husband's "the-dog-has-torn-something-up-again" call.

Hurley sat at her feet and stared with his pitiful brown eyes.

"Come on," she said. "You need to apologize." As she approached the bedroom, an acrid odor made her nostrils flare. "Hurley! Bad boy." She looked around the floor for a mess.

"What's wrong with the toilet? It won't flush." Gary stood in the bathroom looking particularly helpless.

Deena pinched her nose closed with her fingers. "Good grief, Gary. What did you have for lunch?"

"Scott and I tried that new Mongolian restaurant. I had—"

"Don't tell me. I don't want to know." Her eyes watered as she backed into the bedroom. Still holding her nose, she added, "Russell turned off the water to fix the disposer."

Gary followed her out. "Oh, good then. I'll just turn it back on."

"You can't," she said with a nasally twang. "Something under the faucet in the kitchen is broken. He won't be able to fix it."

Gary fanned his face. "Got it. I know what to do." He headed to the other side of the house.

Trying to hold her breath wouldn't work, so Deena began breathing out of her mouth. She grabbed a bath towel and sat on the floor, pushing the edge of it under her closet door.

Gary came in carrying the orange plastic bucket from the garage that he used to wash his car. "What are you doing?"

"I'm protecting my clothes from that stench. If it leaks into my closet, I'm going to have to buy a whole new wardrobe."

"C'mon. It's not that bad."

Deena shot him a look that made it obvious she didn't agree. "What are you doing?"

"I'm going to get water from the backyard and pour it into the tank so it will flush."

"From where in the backyard?"

"The water hose."

"It's a good thing you're pretty," Deena chuckled. "The water is turned off there, too, remember?"

Gary threw back his head. "I guess I could go over to Edwin Cooper's house and ask to borrow a bucket of water."

"Or you could get it out of the cement pond in the backyard."

"The swimming pool? Right."

Gary went to the backyard with Hurley right behind.

It was pretty bad when a dog had to escape an odor. Deena shoved the last bit of towel under the closet door and hurried out of the bedroom, shutting the door securely behind her. Once back in her office, she closed the French doors and took a deep breath.

She had lost her appetite for supper. Her computer was in sleep mode, and she went back to her quest. What did this Houston murder have to do with Alexis Dekker, and who was this new possible suspect? More importantly, would it be enough to get Detective Guttman off Cliff's back?

She read through the article again, this time more slowly. The quote from the victim's husband was just the clue she was looking for.

Now that she had a lead, she needed to look for follow-up stories. She would call Ian in the morning to ask if she was on the right track. For now, she wanted to share the news with Russell. She reached for her phone and fired off a text message.

Maybe he would be as hopeful as she was.

Chapter 9

Russell Sinclair sat outside on the front steps as he waited for Cliff to pick him up from Estelle's house. Even though they had been married for months, he still considered the large Victorian house on the outskirts of Maycroft as his wife's. After all, people in town still referred to it as Fitzhugh Manor and probably always would.

Cliff had volunteered to meet Russell and bring him the replacement garbage disposal for Deena since he needed to do some shopping anyway.

Unlike Russell, Cliff was usually on time. Today, though, he was running late. Russell checked his cell phone in case he had missed a message. There was one from Deena. He pulled his readers out of his shirt pocket and read it through several times. "Found a new insect. Cliff could be infected."

What the heck? He dialed Deena's cell number, remembering how she crabbed on him about calling her home phone.

When she answered, he asked about the cryptic message.

"What? That's not what I wrote," she said. "I wrote, 'Found a new suspect. Cliff might be acquitted.'"

Russell laughed. "I've been telling you it's time for new reading glasses. Between auto-correct and your poor eyesight, you should be careful about what you type. You almost started an epidemic."

The annoyance in Deena's voice came through the cyber wire. "I don't need glasses. I can see perfectly well. It's just this phone. The letters are too—"

"Hey. Cliff's here. I'll call you later." He hung up as Cliff's truck came bumping down the long drive that led to the front of the house. Russell had decided that today there would be no talk of Alexis Dekker or murder or lawyers, unless Cliff brought it up.

Russell stood and stretched his legs. He picked up his toolbox and got in the front seat. He leaned over the seat to set the tools in the backseat. There on the floorboard, the tips of yellow roses peeked out from under an old, greasy towel. The box with the disposer was next to it. Cliff's being late made sense now. He must have stopped off to get flowers to put on his wife's grave.

"You're late," Russell said.

"It's a long way out here to Beverly Hills, ya know." Cliff adjusted his ball cap. It was his going-to-town, fancy John Deere trucker hat.

"Thanks for coming all the way out here. I owe you one."

Cliff glanced at Russell and snickered.

They talked baseball all the way to Deena's house. The Texas Rangers had a chance to clinch the playoffs if they could get past the Mariners. The big series was starting today with an afternoon game.

Cliff pulled up in front of the house. "I'll pick you up in about an hour. Should I get stuff to make sandwiches or will one of your fancy servants be making lunch?"

Russell blushed. He was still adjusting to being a working-class guy living a millionaire's life. "The housekeeper will take care of it." He reached in the backseat.

"I'll get it," Cliff said and quickly jumped out of the truck to open the back door. He pulled out the toolbox and disposer and walked around to hand them to Russell. "Don't forget to turn that ring counterclockwise to make sure it seats correctly."

"Sure thing, boss." Russell headed toward the front door and rang the bell. As Cliff drove away, he wondered why his friend would keep the flowers and cemetery visit a secret. They usually told each other everything. Then, a few weeks back, Russell had mentioned the idea of setting Cliff up on a double date with a woman in Estelle's Bluebonnet Club, and Cliff had gone ballistic.

Russell had never seen him so mad. He dropped the subject immediately. It had been three years since cancer took Gail, and Cliff still couldn't seem to stomach the thought of being with another woman.

Russell shook his head. *That's a far cry from Max Dekker.* From what Deena said, he was moving on to another woman in less than three days.

Deena opened the door. A look of relief covered her face.

* * *

"I'M SO GLAD YOU'RE here," Deena said. "I'm not meant for pioneer life. And Gary...he wouldn't survive a week in the little house on the prairie."

Russell headed straight to the kitchen. "Sorry to hear that. What are you going to do when some cyber-attack knocks out the power grid and the entire country is in a state of emergency? You really should be prepared with at least the basics."

"We'll come hide in the bunker with you and Cliff, I suppose. And by 'we' I mean Hurley and I. Gary will be too freaked out to live with. I'll bring the caviar and champagne."

Russell knew she was making fun of him, but he took preparedness seriously. He had survived sixty-something years already and wasn't about to let the zombie apocalypse get the better of him. He headed straight to the kitchen to get to work.

Deena sat at the kitchen counter. "So do you want to hear about the new suspect?

Russell tried to hide his annoyance from her previous remarks. "Sure."

"Well, about five years ago, a street gang in Houston set up an initiation for new members. They had to kill a person by...by...well—I'm not going to say. It's too gruesome. But apparently, the circumstances were very similar to the plot in one of Max Dekker's novels, *Bounty Beyond the Border.* Have you read it?"

Russell reached for his pliers and bumped his head on the edge of the cabinet. "Geez." He rubbed the spot. "You know I don't read fiction."

Without even looking, he knew Deena was rolling her eyes.

"If you call conspiracy theories 'non-fiction.'"

He let the comment pass this time.

"Anyway, the husband of the woman who was killed blamed Max and filed a lawsuit. It was settled immediately, but the man said he still vowed revenge."

Russell sat up on the kitchen floor. "One problem, Sherlock. If he wanted revenge, why didn't he go after Max instead of Alexis?"

"Because, Watson, he wanted Max to suffer the loss of his wife just like he had. Only it looks like the plan failed since Max Dekker already has another love interest."

"Hmm. Interesting theory. Did you tell Ian?"

"Actually, Ian already knew about it. I talked to him this morning. He said that the police are checking on the guy's alibi for the night of the murder. In the meantime, they've taken their focus off Cliff."

"That's great news." He stood and wiped his hands on a rag he pulled from his toolbox. "And so is this." He flipped the switch and the disposer purred like a kitten.

"Hooray! You're a genius."

"Let me just change out this valve handle, and I can get your water turned back on."

Deena's cell phone rang and she walked away from the kitchen to answer it.

Russell wasn't worried about Cliff being charged with murder, even if there was an over-zealous detective on the case. Ian was a smart lawyer, and there was no physical evidence to tie him to the crime. Then he pictured the pocketknife on the top of the refrigerator. Coincidence. He dismissed the thought from his mind.

He was, however, worried about his friend's mental state. Maybe he needed to see someone. Counseling had been a lifesaver for Russell with his PTSD. Maybe he should suggest it to Cliff.

He tightened the handle under the sink and slid out from underneath the cabinet. When he stood, he looked over to see Deena. The look on her face reminded him of the time they saw *Jaws* together at the theater.

"What is it? What's wrong?"

"That was Ian," she said slowly. "The man from Houston has disappeared. They think he may be in Maycroft."

* * *

RUSSELL SET HIS TOOLBOX and the used disposer in the bed of Cliff's pick-up. They could use the old one for parts. He climbed into the passenger seat and greeted a smiling Cliff.

Deena's neighbor, Christy Ann something-or-other, waved at them from her driveway. Cliff tipped his cap as they drove by.

"You seem like you're in a good mood," Russell said as he turned down the radio.

"I guess I am." Cliff adjusted his cap.

"So you're not worrying about..."

"That police mess? Nah. I have a good lawyer and a clear conscience. That should be enough in the good ol' U.S. of A."

Russell sat up straight so he could glance into the back seat. Sure enough, the flowers were gone. Then he noticed something else. "Hey, where are your groceries? Did you walk out and leave them at the store?"

"Umm...I couldn't find anything I wanted. That's all." His tone had turned sour on a dime.

"Not even beer? I thought you said you were out."

Cliff shifted in his seat. "It was too dang expensive, okay. I'll pick some up at the corner store on my way home." He set his jaw. "And quit needling me. You're worse than a nagging wife."

Wife. That must be the problem. He just couln't let go of Gail.

They drove for a few minutes in silence. Russell finally got up the nerve to broach the subject. "Look, Cliff. I know it's hard losing Gail."

"Gail? What does she have to do with anything?"

"I know you went to the cemetery. I saw the flowers."

If steam could actually pour out of a person's ears, Cliff would have been lit up like a locomotive. His face turned a purplish shade of red and his eyes narrowed to tiny slits. "Look, man, what I do is my business. Not yours. You just need to leave me alone. And besides, what would you know about how I feel? You just found the love of your life."

Russell knew by the way he gritted his teeth that Cliff was holding back more. "Sorry. I'm just trying to help."

Cliff turned down the driveway and slammed on the brakes in front of Estelle's house.

Russell got out. When he saw Cliff sitting rigid, he knew he'd over-stepped his boundaries again. "Aren't you coming in to watch the game?"

"Not today. Ain't in the mood."

There was no use pleading with him at this point. Cliff needed time to cool off. He closed the truck door as his friend peeled out toward the main road.

Estelle opened the front door decked out in her best Texas Rangers fan apparel. A gift from Russell. Her eyes followed

Cliff's truck as he sped off. "I thought we were all going to watch the game together."

"We had a fight." Russell stepped past Estelle and went into the house. As he settled down into the man cave—formerly the parlor—he couldn't get the look of Cliff's face out of his mind. He had seen Cliff upset, mad, annoyed, hot under the collar—plenty of times. But this was the first time he had seen him enraged.

Was it possible that Cliff was suffering from depression? He hadn't been himself lately. Russell closed his eyes and rubbed them with his hands.

That day at the salon, maybe something in Cliff snapped. Maybe he *did* get mad and cut that woman's brake line. One thing was for sure, when he drove off just now, he had a look on his face of a man capable of anything.

Chapter 10

Deena could still remember the first time she showed up unexpectedly at Gary's office. She had just come from the doctor, thinking that she had the flu. They had only been married three months.

He had been surprised to see her and even a little nervous he might get in hot water with the boss. That was when he was the newest employee in a small CPA firm in North Dallas.

Deena shook her head as though shooing away a wasp and looked at the clock on her dashboard. It was almost four o'clock on Friday afternoon. His clients would all be gone, and he and his co-workers would have already loosened their ties or kicked up their heels. Their computers would be shut down and the main topic of conversation would likely be sports or shopping or plans to go to the lake or barbecuing in the backyard.

It was the perfect time to ask Gary to do something he would dread.

Deena had wrapped an ice-cold bottle of one of those Texas craft beers he was crazy about in aluminum foil and had stuck it in her purse.

Sheila, the chatty receptionist, was away from her desk. Deena could see Gary's door open, so she went back and stuck her head inside.

"Knock, knock." Gary was talking to his friend Scott, who had his feet stretched out and hands locked behind his head.

"Hey, Deena," Scott said, quickly sitting up.

"Don't get up," she said, meeting Gary's smiling eyes. "I just stopped by to see the two most handsome financial geniuses in all of Perry County."

"Oh," Gary said. "In that case, I'll go get Richie."

"Ha!" She walked over to him, planting a kiss on his cheek.

Scott folded up his long legs and stood. "Well, I guess I'll let you two love-birds have your privacy. Call me about Sunday."

Gary gave him a "bro nod" with his chin. After Scott left, Gary smiled at Deena. "So what brings you all the way downtown from suburbia?"

"This." She pulled out the bottle and unwrapped the foil.

Gary practically squealed with delight as he unscrewed the lid and took a long chug. He let out a satisfying "Ahh" sound. "I am either the luckiest man in the world, or you have a favor to ask."

Deena scrunched up her nose. Was she that obvious? "Why can't it be both?"

"It can be. Besides, I have a favor to ask, too."

"Sunday. Golfing with Scott?" she asked.

"Yep. If it's okay with you."

"Sure. Anything for my super sweet, hunky husband."

"Uh-oh. I have a feeling this is going to cost me. What?"

"My favor will only take about an hour of your time."

Gary winked and shook his head. "You got it, babe."

"Not that!" she said, pretending to be shocked. She paused. "Tomorrow is the memorial for Alexis Dekker. I want to go."

"What?" Gary nearly tipped out of his chair. Beer spilled onto his shirt. "Why on earth would you want to go? Have you forgotten that you are under suspicion for murder or accessory to murder or something?" He used his handkerchief to wipe his shirt and tie.

"First of all, I'm sure everything got cleared up when Detective Guttman talked to Betty. Second of all, that's exactly why I need to be there. I need to show everyone I'm *not* guilty. If I stay away, it might look like I have something to hide."

"That sounds like 'Mystery of the Week' hogwash. This is real life, Deena Jo. You never go back to the scene of the crime."

"And what show did you get that from?" She could see his point, of course. But what she didn't say was that she wanted to get a better feel for Max Dekker's guilt or innocence. Maybe she would see the mysterious mistress. Maybe the copycat victim's widower would show up. Instead, she said with a softer tone, "You trust me, don't you?"

Gary threw his wet handkerchief in his top drawer. He rested both elbows on the desk and leaned his chin on his folded hands. "In this case, no, I don't. You aren't thinking straight, and I think I know why."

Here he goes. Gary was trying to play shrink with her again. She crossed her arms and waited.

"Ever since we were first married, you've always been on a mission to save somebody. First, it was Russell and then me and then your various misfit students. Lately, it's been Estelle, then Katy, and now Cliff."

"What can I say? I'm a caring person."

"It seems to go beyond that with you. It's an obsession." He folded his arms across his desk.

She jumped from her seat. "Forget about it. I'll ask Russell to go. He doesn't try to psychoanalyze me all the time." She stormed out of his office despite the protests she could hear from behind her.

As soon as she started up the car, her anger slipped into sorrow and dripped onto her blouse. She knew Gary was just worried about her, so why couldn't he just say so? It wasn't as if she were planning on buying herself a motorcycle or anything. She just wanted to see what was up with the Dekker case.

It would be a long, chilly evening in the Sharpe house.

Chapter 11

Deena insisted on driving so she wouldn't get her nice "funeral dress" dirty in Russell's truck. She hadn't worn heels in a while—even to church—and she wondered if her feet had grown a size. She would have to make do for one hour until she could slip back into her comfy Toms.

She and Gary had made up the night before. They subscribed to the never-go-to-bed-mad philosophy of a healthy marriage. He had even offered to go with her to the memorial service. Still, there was tension between them.

When she picked up Russell, he looked uncomfortable in his dress slacks and tie. He had cut himself shaving and had a spot of blood on his chin.

Deena licked her thumb and rubbed it clean.

"Stop!" Russell jerked his head away and pulled down the visor mirror to look at his wound.

"Sorry. Maternal instinct."

"So what exactly do you hope to get out of this shindig besides seeing a bunch of rich, snobby New Yorkers?"

Deena shook her head. "You're rich, and you're not snobby."

"I'm the exception—not the rule."

"Well, for one, I want to size up Max Dekker and see if he truly is the grieving widower he should be. Maybe we'll find out who that other woman is."

"What about that guy from Houston? What if he comes in with guns blazing? I don't want to have to take a bullet for you, but I will."

"Thanks, but I'm sure there will be security there. Ian said that they are on the lookout for the guy."

"Do you know what he looks like?"

"No. There wasn't a picture of him in that newspaper article I read. Only his wife. His name is Joseph Ramos."

Visitation had already started when they pulled up to Mortimer's Funeral Home. Deena had not wanted to be among the first to arrive. A black Hummer limo, not a common sight in Maycroft, was parked near the entrance. A handful of other cars dotted the parking lot.

Standing off to the side of the building under the shade of an oak tree was Detective Guttman. He nodded his head at Deena when she got out of the car.

"Good. Guttman sees us," Deena said, nodding her head in his direction.

"So that's the new sheriff in town," Russell said. "I need to talk to him."

"No, you don't. And he's a detective, not the sheriff." She took Russell's arm and steered him toward the entrance.

This was not the first time Deena had been inside Mortimer's. It was Maycroft's best-known funeral home. Jeffrey Mortimer stood inside the door directing visitors to sign the guestbook and passing out programs. She looked past him to see a small gathering down front. A few people were already seated and some were on their cell phones. Must be the New York crowd.

She signed the book with a larger than normal signature and scanned the short list of names for any she recognized. There was one. Charla Hicks.

As soon as she and Russell entered the main chapel, Deena spotted the biggest, blondest hair in the Southwest rush toward her.

Charla grabbed Deena as though they were best friends and gave her a double-cheek air kiss. "Can you believe it? What a tragedy! You know I sold them their house."

As Maycroft's most ambitious realtor, Deena wasn't at all surprised that Charla had been involved with Maycroft's only celebrity couple. What she couldn't believe was how high Charla's hair was coifed. In fact, she couldn't help but stare. That hair needed its own zip code.

Charla got the message. "Oh, my hair." She reached up to pat the top. "I know. Of all times for Melissa to go on vacation. I had to get it done by someone else. Is it sticking up too high?"

"Um, no. It looks fine," Deena lied. "You say Melissa is on vacation?"

"That's right. Took off without telling a soul."

Deena hated stating the obvious, but she couldn't resist. "Is she the one who—"

"Last saw Alexis Dekker alive? You bet your booty." Charla turned to Russell. "Hi, I'm Charla Hicks. You must be Deena's brother I've heard so much about. I don't believe we've met." She batted her eyes and held out her hand as though Russell were supposed to kiss it.

He reached up and shook it awkwardly. "Russell Sinclair."

In a flash, Charla handed Russell her business card. "Call me if you're interested in buying another mansion. Maybe something in the city on the lake." With that, she turned and headed off to greet the next potential customer.

Russell dropped the card in a waste can and followed Deena down the aisle toward Max Dekker.

A beautiful blue cloisonné urn sat in the middle of a long table surrounded by more pots of flowers than she had ever seen in one place. Purple hydrangeas, white lilies, and yellow roses were overpowering in looks and scent.

As they approached, Max spotted her through an opening in the crowd and walked to where she stood waiting. "Mrs. Sharpe. Here to finish off the job?" he asked when he got near enough to speak.

Deena held out her hand. "Now you know better than that, Mr. Dekker. I'm here to offer my condolences, just like I planned to do the other day when there was that...unfortunate incident at your house."

"Unfortunate incident." He paused. "Interesting choice of words."

"This is my brother, Russell Sinclair."

The two men shook hands.

"Sorry for your loss," Russell said, just like Deena had coached him.

"Ah. You are the friend of my wife's suspected killer."

Russell opened his mouth to speak, but Deena held up her hand to stop him.

"Now Mr. Dekker, you know good and well that neither I nor our friend had anything to do with your wife's death. Besides, this is no place for a conversation like that."

She looked into his deep, blue eyes and saw a mixture of what was surely grief and fatigue. These were not the eyes of a killer.

"About that, you are right." He sighed so deeply that Deena worried he would deflate like an old balloon.

"Max, the funeral director needs to speak to you." The woman's voice was connected to another familiar face. It was the same woman Deena had seen just a few days earlier in the bay window of Max Dekker's house.

She smiled at Deena and Russell. "I'm Barbara Conroy. Thank you both so much for coming."

Deena smiled back. She knew the name immediately from the Wikipedia article about Max. Barbara Conroy was his second wife. The one he divorced after two years in order to remarry Alexis.

"Duty calls," Max said and walked toward the back of the room with Barbara.

"I can't believe that," Deena whispered to Russell when the couple was out of earshot. "That's his ex-wife. The woman I saw him kissing."

"Well, that makes sense. She came to visit. He greets her with a kiss."

"It wasn't a 'Hi, how are you?' kind of kiss. Trust me."

The organist began playing a hymn, a cue for everyone to be seated. Deena led Russell toward the back. She wanted a bird's eye view in case anything interesting went down. With luck, there might be some drama.

* * *

THE SERVICE WAS SHORT and simple. Nothing unusual happened, and Deena was slightly disappointed. During most of the service, she couldn't take her eyes off Barbara Conroy.

Barbara was the "Rhoda" to Alexis's "Mary." Whereas the pictures of Alexis showed a stylish, tall, thin, elegant woman with heels that could double as circus stilts, Barbara appeared more genteel and plain-Jane. Deena wouldn't be surprised if Barbara was actually from the South. Barbara could never pull off the designer look of the clothes Deena saw at the thrift shop. She would look like a pig dressed up like a poodle. Instead, she looked comfortable in her department store dress and sensible black pumps. You can tell a lot about a woman by her shoes, you know.

Barbara sat behind Max on the second row. The first row seemed filled with brothers, sisters, or cousins. Most of the folks looked to be in their sixties, about the same age as Max. Barbara stood and sat on cue with the pastor, bowing her head appropriately.

Deena wondered what she was actually thinking. Was she delighted to be rid of her archrival? Would she be moving in shortly with her ex-husband? Everyone kept secrets; no one knew that better than Deena. What deep, dark secrets was Barbara Conroy keeping and would they somehow explain the mystery of the murder of Alexis Dekker?

When the service ended, Deena and Russell hurried out. They didn't want to hang around for chitchat. Russell headed straight out to Detective Guttman who was still holding up the old oak tree. Deena tried to catch up with him, but her Sunday heels made it impossible.

"Detective Guttman, I'm Russell Sinclair. I'm a friend of Cliff Abel's. I'm his *best* friend, that is."

Guttman twirled the toothpick hanging out of the corner of his mouth and gave Russell a sideways stare. He looked at Deena. "Is this guy with you?"

"Yes," Deena said. "He's my brother."

"I see. So, what can I do for you, Mr. Sinclair?"

"You can leave my friend alone. He didn't kill anybody. He's not that kind of person."

The detective chuckled and threw the toothpick on the ground. "And I guess I'm just supposed to take your word for that, huh?"

Russell jammed his hands deep in his pockets. "No, but you should take character witnesses into account. That should mean something."

"Look, Mr. Sinclair. I'm a detective. We deal in facts and evidence. When I get all the facts of this case together, I'll know if your buddy Cliff is guilty or not."

"What about Melissa?" Deena asked. "She's Mrs. Dekker's hairstylist."

"We talked to her. We don't consider her a suspect."

"Did you know she's missing?"

"Missing? What do you mean?" Guttman's eyes narrowed.

"Apparently, she took off without telling anyone she was leaving." Deena stared down the detective.

"Maybe it's a coincidence. Or maybe she's dealing with personal issues. After all, she was the last person to see Alexis Dekker alive."

"Exactly!" Deena folded her arms.

"Look here, Mrs. Sharpe. If I were you, I'd quit trying to play amateur sleuth and worry about your own alibi."

"Is that a threat?" Russell leaned in, his fists balled in his pockets.

"Not at all," Guttman said. "It's just that Mrs. Sharpe here still has some explaining to do."

"Me?" Deena didn't disguise the surprise in her voice. "What are you talking about?"

"Your alibi for going to Max Dekker's house on Wednesday didn't pan out."

"You mean Betty Donaldson and Lydia Ivey? Did you talk to them?"

"I didn't need to talk to Ms. Ivey. Mrs. Donaldson made it clear that she didn't go with you to the Dekker house. I was planning on calling you back for another interview as soon as I chase down some other information."

Deena's mouth dropped open. She couldn't believe that Betty had lied about that day. Her surprise quickly turned to anger. She measured her words carefully. "So how did you know I—I mean we—had been at the house?"

"Max Dekker reported seeing you and recognized you from the writing class."

Deena fumed. "I can assure you, Detective, that Mrs. Donaldson was indeed there that day. I can also assure you that you will be hearing from her shortly."

Deena pulled on Russell's arm and turned toward the parking lot.

"Mrs. Sharpe," Guttman called after her. "A coerced confession is a false confession. It'll never stand up in court."

She wanted to scream. She needed to take action. After dropping Russell off, she would drive straight to Betty's house and confront that little snippet. Before this day was over, her name would be cleared if it was the last thing she did.

Russell broke her tunnel vision. "Slow down!"

Deena slammed on her brakes.

A man crossing the street jumped to avoid getting hit. He glared at her then trotted off down the street that ran beside the funeral home.

Deena took a couple of deep breaths to steady her nerves. "I'm sorry. That was close."

"Just be careful," Russell said. "We don't need any more casualties."

Deena looked both ways twice before proceeding down the road. "Did you recognize that guy?"

Russell clenched the handle above the door. "No, but he looked familiar. Must live around here."

"I feel like I've seen him before." As she drove toward Estelle's house, she tried to remember where she had seen that face. By his silence, she supposed Russell was trying to figure it out, too.

* * *

DEENA AND BETTY WEREN'T exactly what you'd call bosom buddies. In fact, Deena had never been to Betty's house.

When the snarky librarian opened the door, Deena was surprised to see her in her bathrobe. After all, it was Saturday afternoon. She wondered if Betty had not changed clothes from the morning or if she had already changed for the evening.

"Deena?"

"Can I come in? I need to talk to you." Deena didn't wait for an answer. She pushed her way into the foyer. She could see past the entry into the den where Betty's husband, Phil, was reading in an easy chair. Deena had known for a while now that Betty suspected him of cheating on her. The rumor had made its way through the small town. She could see why. Phil could have been a stand-in for Cary Grant. He waved to her and went back to his magazine.

Betty led Deena into the study or library or office. Everybody has their own name for the room with sparse seating but ample books. "Wait here," Betty said, and left to go down the hall toward the bedrooms.

Deena was too impatient to sit. She walked over to the tidy shelves and scanned the book titles. An impressive array of fiction and non-fiction stared back at her. It didn't take her long to realize that the books were arranged by author name. Once a librarian, always a librarian. Deena spotted the section with Max Dekker's books. It looked like Betty must have one of every novel he'd ever written. Except, that is, for his first book, *Crimson Waters*. She had two copies of that one.

It was the book she had asked him to sign on Monday in class. Deena slid the book out of its spot and opened it to the title page. Instead of being autographed to Betty, the inscription was addressed to someone named Lizzie Bogmire. Max had signed it and dated it December 1, 1977.

She reached for the second copy when Betty returned wearing one of her signature pantsuits. The fabric was crumpled and had probably come straight out of the laundry hamper.

"You didn't need to dress up for me," Deena stated flatly. "I don't plan on being here that long." She held up the book. "By the way, who is Lizzie Bogmire?"

Betty's mouth tightened, but her eyes remained fixed on Deena. "My sister." She paused and then added, "She's dead."

"Oh, I'm so sorry." Deena pushed the book back into its rightful place.

"Why did you go to the memorial, and why are you here, dear?" Betty's eyes danced back and forth between Deena and the bookshelf.

"How do you know I went to the memorial?"

"Seems obvious. Most people don't wear a black dress and heels in the middle of a Saturday afternoon."

"What did you tell Detective Guttman about our visit to Max Dekker's house? Or better yet, what *didn't* you tell him?" Deena stood rigidly, wanting a straight answer.

Betty glided past her to the shelf. "I simply answered his questions. I told the truth." She adjusted the book Deena had handled, making sure it lined up exactly with the others on the shelf. She pulled and pushed a few more times until she was satisfied with its position.

Deena sat on the small sofa. "So what did he ask, and what did you say?"

Betty stood with her back to the shelf. "He asked me if I had driven out to Max Dekker's house on Wednesday, and I told him the truth."

Deena shook her head. "Then why did he say you didn't verify my story that we went there to take food and offer condolences?"

"Beats me. I guess you'd have to ask him that question." Betty sat down in the Queen Anne style chair, her back ramrod straight. It made her pointy features look sharp enough to slice meat.

"Did you tell him about seeing Max kiss that other woman?"

Betty hesitated. "No."

"Which part, no?"

She blew out her breath and looked a mile past Deena at the far wall. "All of it."

"I don't understand. You said he asked you if you went to Max Dekker's house and you said yes."

Betty stood and wrung her hands. "That's not what I said." She stared at her hands as if the words were written on them. "He asked if I *drove* to Max Dekker's house on Wednesday, and I said no. That was the truth. *You* drove, not me."

Deena leaped off the sofa. "What? Now you're parsing words? Do you realize how that makes me look?"

Betty walked to the window and stared out through the curtains. "I suppose. It's just that I've read enough murder mysteries to know that you never talk to the police. They aren't looking for the truth—they just want a conviction."

"Betty, you can't really believe that." Deena took a step closer.

Betty turned around and stuck out her chin. "I can and I do."

"Well, regardless, you are going to call Detective Guttman and tell him everything that happened."

Betty stood defiant.

"Do you want me to walk in there and tell Phil what you did?" The threat seemed to get her attention, like a small child afraid to get in trouble with daddy.

"Oh-all-right." She spat out the words. "I'll call him on Monday."

"Not Monday. Now!" Deena pulled out her cell phone and pursed her lips. "I want to hear every last word you say to him. And don't leave anything out this time."

Betty looked at the phone and then down the hall toward the den. She walked over and quietly closed the doors of the study while Deena called the number.

"Detective Guttman," Deena said, "I'm here with Betty Donaldson, and she has something to tell you."

Chapter 12

Satisfied that Guttman now had all the facts on her, she drove to the Hidden Treasures Antique Mall to check on her booth. Actually, she was stalling before going home to see Gary. His words still stung.

She shook her head to get the words away from her. They were just too painful.

Janet had filled the front window of the shop with nostalgic, fall-related items. Pumpkins, baskets with orange and yellow leaves, and a scarecrow highlighted the bits of furniture and knick-knacks cleverly arranged in a small vignette. She clearly had a knack for decorating.

"Hey, girlfriend," Janet called out when she came through the door. "What are you all dressed up for?"

"I've just come from the memorial for Alexis Dekker."

"Oh. I didn't realize you knew her."

"I didn't, actually. I know Max Dekker. He's teaching a class at the library."

Janet tsk-tsked. "So tragic. It makes me think about closing the shop and moving off to Florida to enjoy my golden years before something terrible happens."

"You can't do that. We need you here. Besides, you have lots of years ahead of you still."

"So did Alexis Dekker."

Deena offered up a conciliatory smile and headed down the main aisle to her booth.

Funerals have a way of making people take stock of their own lives, to reflect on their own mortality. Since both her parents were still alive, Deena believed she had many years left to live.

When her father had a minor heart attack a few years back, she had been so scared for him, but she was also scared for herself. If anything happened to her parents, she would be the matriarch of the family. Because neither she nor Russell had children, she would technically be the end of the line.

She looked around her small booth at all her wares. For some reason, they seemed to have lost their appeal. The glassware had less sparkle, and the pottery seemed faded and lackluster. All at once, she had a strong desire to be home. To be in Gary's safe, comforting arms. She grabbed her purse and headed toward the exit.

The air outside had turned cold as clouds barricaded the sun.

Her cell phone rang as she got into her car. She hoped it was Gary. Instead, it was Ian.

"What are you doing working on a Saturday?" she asked, knowing this wasn't likely a social call.

"I just got a call from Detective Guttman. He said your story checked out, and you are no longer considered a 'person of interest' in the case."

She started up the car and turned on the heater. "It's about time."

"There's another concern with Cliff though."

"Uh-oh."

"They talked to the night watchman at the cemetery who said he remembered seeing Cliff arrive a few minutes after he went on duty at seven o'clock. The problem is that the hairdresser had said he left the shop about a quarter after six. Given the driving time, there's a thirty-minute gap from when he left the salon to when he got to the cemetery."

"Yikes. That's a good bit of time."

"Precisely. Maybe you and Russell can get him to tell you what he was doing during that half hour."

"I'll see what I can do." She promised to let him know if she found out anything.

She was anxious to get home. Her legs were cold and her feet hurt from wearing heels all morning. She took off her shoes and laid them on the passenger seat. She couldn't wait to see Gary, eat a sandwich, and curl up next to him to watch the baseball game and read a book. Maybe later she would have another go at making divinity.

When she stopped at the light, she dialed Russell's number. Her SUV was equipped with Bluetooth, but she'd never quite figured out how to make it work.

"Are you planning to see Cliff today?" she asked her brother when he answered.

"That's unlikely." Russell explained the altercation he had with Cliff.

"Wow. Sounds like he's really coming unhinged." She then told Russell about her conversation with Ian. "I think we need to ask him directly what happened during that gap in time."

"You can ask him, then. I don't want to stir that wasp's nest again."

"If only we could locate that guy who helped him out. I assume you haven't gotten any calls from those businesses."

"Nope. I remember when Maycroft was such a small town that everybody knew each other. Not that way anymore. Maybe we should get more copies of the picture and put them up around town."

"Maybe." Deena heard a gasp on the other end of the line. "Russell? Are you okay?"

"I got it! The guy we saw in the street today. It was the guy in the picture!"

Deena pulled the car over to the side of the road. "Are you sure?" She opened the glove compartment and pulled out the drawing. "You're right! I have it right here."

"Do you think he lives in that part of town? Do you think he was at the memorial?"

"I doubt he was at the memorial," Deena said. "He was wearing jeans and a ball cap. I've got an idea. I'm going to take this picture to Guttman and see if they can track this guy down. They're the cops. It's their job, right?"

"Seems to me they are usually more helpful in tracking down the bad guys than clearing the good guys, but I guess it wouldn't hurt. I just hope whatever the guy has to say doesn't come back to bite Cliff."

Deena hadn't thought about that. But at this point, she just wanted to get to the truth.

* * *

SNUGGLING WITH GARY would have to wait. She called Guttman who was, not surprisingly, still in his office. He told her to come by and show him the picture.

The receptionist led her back to Guttman's office.

Deena was surprised when he stood to greet her.

"Glad you stopped by, Mrs. Sharpe. I talked to your attorney and told him your story checked out."

"Yes, he called me. Thanks." She wondered why she was thanking him since she hadn't done anything wrong in the first place.

"I have a few questions for you about the salon and that hairstylist, Melissa Engels."

"Before we get into that, I wanted you to look at this picture." She pulled it from her purse.

"Oh, right. The picture."

"This is a drawing my brother made from Cliff's description of the guy who helped him load the wine cooler into Mrs. Dekker's car." She passed the paper across the desk. "We saw him again this afternoon across the street from the funeral home. Maybe someone here will recognize him or be able to track him down."

Guttman's mouth twitched as he looked at the picture. "You say you saw this man today by the funeral home?"

"Yes. Do you know him?"

Guttman laid the picture on the desk and thumbed through a stack of folders on the credenza. He found the one he wanted and opened it. He pulled out a photograph and showed it to Deena. "Is this the man you saw today?"

It was a small mug shot. Deena squinted to focus her eyes on the man's face. Clearly, it was the same person she had seen earlier. "Yes. That's him. Who is he?"

Guttman took back the photo and picked up the phone. He punched a red button. "Get me the captain, pronto." He hung up. His face had turned from stoic to frenzied.

"Mrs. Sharpe, you have been very helpful." He put the picture back into the folder.

"Are you going to tell me who he is?" She couldn't believe he was shooing her away. "Come on Detective, I used to be a reporter. Throw me a bone."

"Sorry, can't. Not yet, anyway." He stood and came around the side of his desk. "I'll be in touch, Mrs. Sharpe. As soon as we have this guy in custody—"

He clamped his mouth shut, obviously having leaked more info than his closed spout had intended. She grinned and headed out the door. No use pushing her luck. She wanted him as an ally. "Thanks," she said again.

She walked out to the parking lot. Someone in a car parked in the back of the lot shrank down in the seat just as she looked that direction. It was her custom to scan her surroundings anytime she was coming or going from a place alone. Lord knows she had preached that to her students often enough. She couldn't tell if the shrinker in the white Ford was a man or a woman. Maybe she should drive a little closer to try to figure out the car's model.

She got in her own car and locked the doors. She was probably just being paranoid. After all, this was the police station. It wouldn't be unusual for someone to want to remain anonymous while parked here. Besides, she had more important things to do.

If the guy she identified to Guttman was about to be tracked down and arrested, she wanted to find out who he was and what he had done. She flashed back to her short stint at the newspaper and the Wilde murder. That gave her an idea. She knew just whom to call.

* * *

CHRISTY ANN WAS IN front of her house planting marigolds with her oldest child. Deena had to admit that her neighbor really was a good mother, even though she could be super annoying and competitive. Maybe Deena should give her a break.

She pulled into the garage and went inside. Just as she thought, Gary was in his recliner watching the baseball game. Hurley was the first to greet her.

"Hey, boy," she said, kneeling and scratching him behind the ears. She looked up at Gary.

He folded down the leg rest of the chair and started to get up.

She stopped him by sitting in his lap and wrapping her arms around his shoulders. "I'm sorry. I don't want to fight anymore."

He squeezed her tight. "You don't have anything to be sorry for. You can't help it that you want to help people. I should admire that, not criticize you for it." He kissed her forehead. "But you are a busy-body, you know."

She laughed and laid her head against his chest. "I know. That's the teacher-reporter-investigator in me."

"I've been thinking about it," Gary said. "Since you retired, it seems like you've been living more on the edge. Been out there and taking risks. It was a lot easier when I knew you were up at the school all day with nothing more dangerous going on than bus duty."

Deena reached for the remote to mute the game. "You know, I never thought of it that way. I only thought about how my retirement affected me, not you. I guess we've both had to make adjustments."

"Don't get me wrong, I love coming home every day to a clean house and a hot meal."

Deena gave him a playful slap on the back of his head. "Ha. If you wanted that, you should have married Christy Ann."

"Speaking of her, she came over looking for you today."

"Did she say why?" Deena got up to let Hurley out the back door.

"Nope. I wouldn't be surprised if she—"

The doorbell sounded right on cue.

"Oh great. Hide your checkbook. Who knows what fund-raiser her kids are involved in now." Deena smoothed out her dress and opened the front door.

"Howdy, neighbor." Christy Ann had her "Miss Teen Maycroft 1998" smile plastered across her face. Her hair was pulled back in a ponytail and her knees showed green stains from kneeling in the grass. Still, she was a beautiful gal.

"What's up? Or rather, how much?"

"What?" The smile slipped from her face, and she tilted her head like Hurley did when you asked him a question.

"I assume you're selling something."

"Actually, no. I came here to offer my help. I heard through the grapevine that you needed some help with baking."

Guilt gripped her by the neck. "Um, uh, come on in." She glanced to the living room at Gary who leaned forward in his chair, pretending to be enraptured by the baseball game.

Christy Ann walked in and looked around. "I see you added French doors to the den."

Very observant. *Is she casing the joint for a burglary?* Deena bit her tongue. Why did she always get so snarky when it came to Christy Ann? "Yes, we did that a few years ago right before I retired. I use it as my office."

"Looks nice."

Deena motioned toward the kitchen table where they both sat. "So how did you hear that I needed help with baking?"

"Through Debbie Lawson at Mommy & Me."

"Who?"

Debbie was at the library for PeeWee StoryTime. She said Nancy, the librarian, had heard something through Betty Donaldson.

"I see. The small town grapevine blossoms again."

"I guess. Anyway, I thought I'd offer to help. You know, baking is one of my specialties."

So is gossiping and meddling. Oops. That's the pot calling the kettle black. "That's really nice of you to offer. I have to make a special cake for Gary's sixtieth birthday party."

"Ooh! I love birthday parties for old people." She clapped her hands. "They're so precious. Almost as sweet as kids' parties."

Did that just happen? Did she somehow invite Christy Ann to Gary's party? And what about that crack about old people? Deena started to say something but stopped herself.

"What kind of cake are we talking about?"

"It's a chocolate swirl divinity cake."

"Hmm. Never heard of it. Do you have a recipe? I can make anything from a recipe."

"Yes, but—"

"When's the party?"

"A week from today." A knot twisted Deena's stomach as she realized she'd done nothing to prepare for the big day.

"Why don't you give me the recipe, and I'll buy all the ingredients. Most people don't realize that brands make a difference. And eggs. Don't even get me started on how one is better than the other. I'll keep a receipt, and you can pay me back." She stood and took a step toward the kitchen. "I suggest we make it on Friday so it has time to rest but is still fresh."

"Sounds good." Deena walked into the kitchen and picked up the recipe box her sister-in-law had given her as a retirement gift. It only had three cards in it. She held it close to her face and pretended to shuffle through a bunch of cards. "Here it is," she said, handing the first card to Christy Ann.

"Super! I'll stop by next week to touch base. Isn't this going to be fun?"

"You betcha!" Deena smiled and walked to the front door. "See ya soon."

Christy Ann looked back over her shoulder. "You know, I knew we had a special bond ever since last year when I saved your brother's life."

Deena waved and shut the door. "And there it is."

"What's that?" Gary asked from the den.

"Nothing. She just can't stop reminding everyone what a hero she was for calling the police on that speeding car. Oh well. At least she's going to help me make your birthday cake. Now I have to figure out a way to bribe her into not telling your mother she helped me."

"That should be easy. Offer to babysit."

"Ugh. I'm not sure which would be worse." She dropped down on the sofa. "I need to get out of this dress. Is it too early to put on pajamas?"

"You haven't told me about the memorial yet."

She slapped her hand against her forehead. "That's right. And the police station."

"What?" Gary turned from the TV.

"Give me a minute to change and make a call, and then I'll tell you all about it."

She got her cell phone and headed to the bedroom. Dan's number was saved in her phone from when they worked together at the newspaper. If anyone would know what was happening with the mystery guy she had identified, Maycroft's top crime reporter would know.

He answered on the second ring.

"Deena Sharpe," he said. "How's it going, cutie?"

"Not too bad. Trying to stay out of trouble."

"That's not what I hear. Your name keeps popping up in regards to the Dekker murder."

Her stomach did a flip-flop. "That's why I'm calling you, actually. I was talking to Detective Guttman today, and I got the impression the info I gave him was important. I think they put an APB out on a guy I identified."

"I heard something like that on the police scanner, but they didn't give a name. They used a code."

"Is there any way you can find out who it is?"

"Sure, but it will take a while. But why are you so interested in this case in the first place? I thought you quit that job with Ian Davis after the Wilde case."

"A guy I know, Cliff Abel, is a suspect."

"Ah. Cliff Abel, the angry appliance repairman. I see."

"He didn't do it."

"I see."

Her face tensed. "Dan, will you help me or not?"

"Yes. I'm actually going out tonight, though, so I'll have to get back with you tomorrow."

"You're going out on a date?"

"Um, yeah. Our first date...we're just friends, though."

"I see," she said and chuckled.

"How about meeting up at our old haunt tomorrow afternoon?"

"Sounds good. See you at one o'clock at the café."

Talking to Dan made her miss being at the newspaper. Maybe she should stop in and say hello to her old boss. Even when he fired her, she knew the editor still liked her. He would probably get a kick out of the idea that she wanted to write mysteries.

However, before she could even think about writing one, she had to solve one. And this case was getting more complex by the day.

She went to her closet and took out the black satchel with the spiral she used for taking notes in class on Monday. She got a pen and opened the notebook to a clean page. In class, Max

Dekker had said to write down anything interesting that you observed or heard around you because it could end up being part of a future book.

At the top of the page, she wrote, "Suspects." She started from the beginning. There was Max Dekker, of course. Like Ian had said, the spouse was always a suspect. Then there was Melissa at the salon. Did she really have a motive? Just because she did not like the woman didn't mean she wanted her dead. She put a question mark next to her name.

Who else? Cliff and his mystery helper. She put an *X* next to Cliff's name. Remembering what Russell had said about Cliff's odd behavior and temper, she scratched out the *X* and changed it to a question mark.

Another suspect was the man from Houston whose wife had been murdered by a local gang. Maybe Dan would know more about him.

One more name kept poking at her brain. It was someone she had wondered about from the beginning but was afraid to contemplate. If he were the killer, what would be the motive? Notoriety? Redemption?

She stared at the blue lines on the paper, and they began to blur. In small letters, she added the name to the list. Linus Guttman.

Chapter 13

"**I took** the liberty of ordering you a club sandwich and sweet tea. Hope that's okay." Dan blew on his coffee before taking a gulp.

Deena noticed he had added cream and sugar to his coffee. Was Dan getting soft? "Perfect." She squeezed a lemon slice into her glass and eyed Dan. His perpetual five o'clock shadow was gone from his face, and he had recently gotten a haircut. More gray was showing, but he looked younger than the average fifty-something. Dating was looking good on him. She didn't dare ask him about it until he had warmed up on a more comfortable topic: murder.

"So, did you find out who my mystery man is?"

His eyes twinkled. "Come on, now. You know how to play this game. You show me yours, and I'll show you mine. How do you know this guy?"

"Fine." She slowly stirred her tea just for a dramatic pause. The dumpy café on the outskirts of town gave her a nostalgic feeling. She had actually missed the sticky red and white checkered tablecloths and the crabby waitress. She proceeded slowly. "My friend, Cliff, went to the salon on Monday to deliver a wine cooler he had repaired for Alexis Dekker. She was supposed to have money to pay him, but didn't."

"Do you mind if I take notes?" Dan asked, reaching into his shirt pocket.

"Just don't quote me. Anyway, he was tired of messing with it, so he went ahead and put it in her car. She had a small sports car with leather seats."

Clara, the waitress who had always served Dan and Deena when they had met there before, brought out the sandwich and refilled Dan's cup.

Deena pulled the toothpick out of the first half. "A man must have seen Cliff struggling to get it in the car and came over to help him. After they got it in, they both drove off."

"So this guy is Cliff's alibi."

"Yes." Deena bit into her sandwich. The answer was actually more complex. Should she tell Dan about the half hour that was still unaccounted for? She decided not to. After all, he was a reporter, and she didn't want to see any more publicity about Cliff's involvement.

"So how do you know this helper?"

"Russell made a sketch of the man from Cliff's description. We showed it around the area businesses, but no one recognized him."

"Do you still have the picture?"

"No, Guttman kept my last copy. But wait...there's more." She took a drink of tea and wiped her mouth.

"Russell and I went to the memorial yesterday."

"I know. I saw you."

"Really? How did I not see you?"

"We reporters know how to stay invisible sometimes. Remember?" He winked.

"So when I was pulling out of the parking lot, I almost hit this guy who was crossing the street. Russell remembered him as the same guy in the sketch. I told Guttman and the rest is history."

"Ahh. So that explains the arrest."

"What does? Who is he?"

It was Dan's turn to play cat and mouse. He added a sugar packet to his coffee and stirred. "I'm only telling you this because it will be public knowledge when the story comes out on Tuesday. I trust you to keep the info under wraps until then." He took a swig. "The man you identified, the man you almost ran over...is a guy from Houston named Joseph Ramos."

"Really? Isn't he the guy whose wife was killed in a copy-cat murder?"

Dan's eyes widened. "You know that already?"

She smiled the smile of someone who had just impressed the unimpressible. "You're not the only one with investigative super-powers around here."

He nodded his head.

"Guttman showed me his mug shot. What was he wanted for?"

"Nothing, until you talked to Guttman. They had checked on his whereabouts after the murder because he had been charged with petty crimes in the past and had been stalking Max Dekker. They couldn't find him."

"So do the police have him in custody now?"

"Yes. He was staying at the Pine Tree Inn outside of town. Get this. Dekker had a restraining order against him, so when you said you saw him outside the funeral home, they nailed him on violating the order. Now they have him locked up until they can make their case against him for the murder."

"So I helped catch another criminal!" She sat back and smiled.

"Looks that way. I have a feeling you and Cliff will be called down to I.D. him tomorrow."

"You mean in a line-up? That's so exciting!"

"Yeah, groovy. Just make sure Guttman doesn't try to pull a fast one. I don't trust that guy."

Those words struck a chord with Deena. "I've been wondering about him." She hesitated, looking down at her plate. "I haven't said this to anyone else, but I was thinking. You have a cop with a reputation for sloppy police work. His uncle pulls some strings and gets him hired as a detective. Then—"

"After just a month of being here, there's a big homicide case to solve."

"So you thought about it, too?"

"Yep. Maybe this guy created his own case to solve in order to rehab his reputation."

Deena clenched her hands. "When you say it out loud, it sounds so much worse."

"I know, but let's talk this through." He lowered his voice. "He has a motive and opportunity. The salon was closed, so there weren't many people around. However, he would need a patsy."

"Plus, he wouldn't want to make it an open and shut case; otherwise, he wouldn't get credit for a big score."

"So who does he frame? The husband is the most likely answer."

Deena leaned in. "But what about Cliff?"

"Too easy. I think he was just in the wrong place at the wrong time. Guttman is probably just using him as a smoke screen. Showing he is turning over lots of stones."

"Then what about Joseph Ramos? Maybe he really did do it to get revenge against Max by killing his wife."

"Maybe." Dan slowly stirred his coffee. "Obviously, he was at the scene, but where's the physical evidence to pin it on him?"

"Or Cliff or Max?"

"Exactly. If Guttman did perpetrate this crime, he might be surprised that all of these suspects are popping up out of the woodwork." He guzzled the last of his coffee. "Hey sugar," he called out to Clara. "Can I get one of these to go?" He waved his empty cup. "Do you need a to-go box?" he asked Deena.

"No. I've lost my appetite."

"Don't worry about this Guttman thing. If he is responsible, we'll catch him. Power of the press and all that." He gave her one of his signature salutes. "By the way, I already knew the first part of your story about the sketch and showing it around. But you got one thing wrong. The little red sports car Alexis was driving. It wasn't hers. It was Max's."

* * *

AS SHE DROVE HOME, her head spun with this new information. Was someone targeting Max but killed Alexis instead? Did this revelation make Max more or less suspicious in the death of his wife? And what about Guttman? Was he a dirty cop trying to clean up his reputation?

She was glad she had talked to Dan. He was a good man, and she felt better knowing he was investigating the case. But talking to him had just confused matters even worse. Maybe Gary was right. She should leave crime solving to the professionals and learn to bake chocolate swirl divinity cake instead.

She laughed aloud when she remembered the last thing Dan had told her. She had finally decided to ask about his love life. Indeed, Maycroft was a small town. She couldn't believe Dan was dating Lydia Ivey. She didn't seem like the most stable post on the porch. Her infatuation with Max Dekker was apparently short lived. At least Lydia would keep Dan living high on the hog with her delicious baked goods.

Deena glanced in the rearview mirror and checked her speed. She had a tendency to drive too fast when she was deep in thought. She tapped her brake pedal to slow down. A white car behind her moved up closer. She held her breath, hoping it wasn't a police car.

It wasn't. It was a Ford sedan.

Chapter 14

They had a reunion, of sorts, on Monday when Deena, Russell, and Cliff all showed up at the police station to identify the stranger. None of them had ever been involved in a line-up, and they were only familiar with it from what they had seen on TV.

The temperature was steadily dropping as fall was introducing itself to Maycroft. The wind howled that early afternoon, and leaves fell like rain from the trees.

Deena was glad she'd grabbed a sweater on the way out.

Russell, seemingly oblivious to the weather, wore his basic cargo shorts and Tommy Bahama floral shirt. Cliff, who was taller and leaner than Russell, wore blue jeans, boots, and a pearl snap shirt. She wondered if he would be going by the cemetery while he was in town.

The temperature inside the police station wasn't much warmer. It might have been the weather, but it was more likely the chill between Russell and Cliff. When would this childish feud end? She tried to make small talk while they waited in the reception area, but both seemed terribly absorbed in the magazines that were strewn across the table.

Mercifully, Guttman didn't keep them waiting long. He led them back to his office and explained how the line-up would work. He would take them back one at a time and then meet with them all again at the end. The attorney for the suspect would be present also.

Guttman took Cliff back first. Another officer waited by the door in the office. Deena pictured herself as a character in a movie about to finger the wrong man. Or worse, what if she didn't recognize anyone?

Russell's leg was bobbing ninety to nothing. He was probably thinking the same thing.

After what seemed forever, but had probably only been about five minutes, Guttman returned. His face revealed nothing. "Who wants to go next?"

Deena looked at Russell. "You go."

He jumped up and followed Guttman out the door.

She pulled out her cell phone. "Is this okay?" she asked the officer.

"Sure. Just don't make any calls."

Deena looked at her phone. No messages. She scrolled through the pictures posted on Facebook. The names were a blur. Maybe Russell was right. Maybe it was time to get glasses. The thought depressed her. She was no more vain than the next person, but the thought of getting glasses just made her feel old.

Gary was turning sixty this week. Her birthday was just around the corner. What was next? Orthopedic shoes and dentures?

Guttman returned. "You're up." He removed his jacket and hung it on the back of his desk chair. He loosened the knot on his tie. If they were playing poker, this might be what card players called a *tell*. But she didn't know him well enough to read him.

Her conversation with Dan came roaring back. Would Guttman lead her into making a false identification or was this not the man he was planning on pinning the murder on?

She followed him to a small dark room with a one-way mirror.

He introduced Mrs. Ortiz, an attorney from Houston. Then he read instructions and noted that the proceedings were being recorded. At last, he announced, "Bring them in," to someone Deena couldn't see.

Six men walked across the back of the room and stopped in front of a wall lined with measurements for height. All were light-skinned Hispanic men about the same build. She instantly recognized the man she had almost run over with her car.

"Do you recognize any one of the people in front you?"

"Yes." The sound of her own voice startled her.

"Can you tell us the number of the person you recognize?"

"Number five."

"And how do you know this person?"

"I saw him crossing the street yesterday by the funeral home. I—I almost hit him with my car."

"Are you sure this was the same man?"

Deena nodded.

"Take them out," Guttman called out to the wizard behind the curtain. He turned to Deena. "Follow me."

He led her back to his office. "I want to thank you all for coming down today. Just so you know, Mrs. Sharpe and Mr. Sinclair identified the same man. Mr. Abel was not able to make a positive identification."

Deena looked at Cliff. "What?"

"A couple of the guys looked similar, but I couldn't be sure. I wish I could."

Guttman patted Cliff's back. "Don't worry about it, Mr. Abel. It happens. We'll check out his whereabouts for that day and see what we can turn up."

Deena studied the detective's face. He was saying the right things, but was he being honest? Could he have left Joseph Ramos out of Cliff's line-up? Impossible. The defendant's lawyer was there, and Guttman said it was being videotaped. Maybe Guttman was on the up-and-up after all.

"Do you think one of those men is the guy who killed that woman?" Cliff asked.

"We're still working on the case. For now, he is being charged with violating a restraining order by being in the same vicinity as Max Dekker."

"Did you ask him about helping me at the salon? What did he say?"

"We did. He denied it, of course. As of now, you are still a person of interest. I hope you understand."

"Whatever." Cliff shuffled his feet. "Are we done here?"

"Yes. You are all free to go. Thank you again for your cooperation."

When they stepped outside, the clouds had blocked out the last rays of sunshine.

Even Russell was feeling the cold now. He crossed his arms. "What do you say we all go get a beer?"

"Too cold for a beer," Deena said, "but you two should go. Grady's is probably open now."

"I got somewhere else to be," Cliff mumbled, heading to his truck.

"Where? The cemetery?" Deena looked around. Did she actually say that?

Cliff shook his head and kept walking.

The cat was out of the bag now. She might as well get it over with. She eyed Russell and then followed Cliff to his truck, opening the passenger side door. She got in and slid over, making room for Russell.

"What the—"

"We want to talk to you, Cliff," Deena said as gently as possible.

"Here? Now?"

"Yes. It's about last Monday." She glanced over at Russell who had lowered his head. Obviously, he wanted her to do the talking. "We know you didn't do anything wrong, and now Detective Guttman knows you didn't either. However, Ian told us that something happened between the salon and the cemetery."

Cliff prickled.

"We're worried about you. Why won't you tell us what happened? We are your friends. You can trust us."

Cliff grabbed his cap from the dashboard and pulled it low down on his head. He glanced past Deena at Russell.

"It's—embarrassing." He waited and so did they. "There's this gal down at the super market. I like her. I think she likes me."

"This is all about a girl?" Russell slapped his knee. "I can't believe it!"

"See? This is why I didn't tell you."

Deena gave Russell her evil stare. "Cliff, I think that's great. We've been hoping you would meet someone. Right, Russell?"

"You bet. But seriously, you're a knot-head for keeping this a secret."

Deena threw back her head. She put her hand on Cliff's arm. "I know this is awkward for you, but—"

"Awkward? It's downright terrifying. I haven't had a date in forty years. Not to mention the guilt."

"Because of Gail?" she asked.

He nodded and stared at his hands. There was still a pale line where his wedding ring used to be.

"Aww, c'mon," Russell said. "You know Gail wanted you to be happy. She said so before she died." He leaned over in front of Deena. "Now who is it? Is it that woman with the long gray hair who looks like she performed at Woodstock?"

A smile crossed Cliff's lips. "Yeah. She's really something. She makes her own jewelry and loves flowers."

"Way to go. She's one hot mama." Russell reached out for a fist bump.

"Ugh. Enough of this guy-talk," Deena said. "So when you left the salon, where did you go?"

"To the market to see Rosemary. Then I went to the cemetery to talk to Gail." His face turned an even brighter shade of pink.

"And when you dropped me off at Deena's to go buy groceries the other day?"

"I was just going to see Rosemary."

Russell let out a hoot. "And all those flowers in the refrigerator at the shop?"

"Those are for the cemetery...mostly. Although Rosemary loves yellow roses. Ruined my pocket-knife cutting all those wet stems."

"Man, I thought you were depressed. I never would have guessed you were in love." He leaned over Deena again. "Have you gotten to second base yet?"

"Time for me to leave. Let me out." Deena scooted toward Russell. "Talk to you guys later. Try to stay out of trouble. And Cliff, call Ian and tell him what you told us."

Before the last word was out of her mouth, Russell had gotten back in the truck.

Cliff drove off and turned in the direction of the sports bar.

Deena dug in her purse for her keys. She got in her car and glanced in the mirror at her hair. The wind had pushed everything over the top and to the left. Then, something behind her caught her attention. She looked back to see a white Ford sedan pulling out of the parking lot. She shuddered, wishing Russell and Cliff hadn't left.

Enough's enough. There was no time to wait. She would have to do this on her own if she wanted to know who was driving that car.

Chapter 15

"I guess it's officially fall," Russell said as he opened the door to Grady's Sports Bar. "Guess I'm gonna have to start wearing pants."

"I absolutely recommend wearing pants in public unless you want to get picked up for flashing," Cliff said. "Want to sit at the bar or in a booth?"

The inside was warm and smelled like stale cigarette smoke. Except for the big-screen TV over the bar, the place was dark. Not unusual for a Monday afternoon.

"The bar. Looks like there's a game on."

They headed for stools at the far end of the bar. Russell recognized the only other man sitting there as Dan Carson, the crime reporter for the newspaper. They met once when Deena had been working with him. "I changed my mind." He led the way to a booth.

"What's up?" Cliff asked as he sat down.

Russell cocked his head toward the bar. "Reporter. We don't need him creepin' in on our conversation."

"Good idea. I'll get us a couple of longnecks and be right back."

Russell's phone vibrated in his pocket. He took it out and looked at the number, but didn't recognize it. He put the phone back in his pocket.

Cliff returned with their drinks. "I scored us some peanuts, too."

Russell held his bottle in front of him. "Let's toast. Here's to friendship and freedom."

Cliff tapped his bottle against Russell's. "I'm not so sure about freedom. Did you see the way that cop looked at me? He was not happy when I couldn't pick out any of those guys."

"Yeah, about that. How were Deena and I able to I.D. him but you weren't?"

"I don't know. Maybe it was a different guy."

"But the picture. It looked just like the guy you described."

"It was close, but not perfect." Cliff took a drink. "Why do you suppose they put only Hispanic guys in the line-up?"

Russell nearly choked on a handful of peanuts. He grabbed his drink to wash them down and cleared his throat. "Um, probably because you said he was Hispanic."

"No I didn't."

"Yes you did. That's how I drew him."

"I never said that. I said he had dark skin. You know, like someone who works out in the sun."

Russell sat back. "Well that explains it. Deena said the guy we saw was named Ramos. Maybe it *wasn't* the same man who helped you that day at the salon."

Russell's phone vibrated again. He pulled it out. Whoever called had left a message. "Let me check this," he said. He held the phone to his good ear. His hearing in the other ear had been damaged in Vietnam. His eyes widened as he listened to the message. When it ended, he picked up his bottle and took a big chug. "We gotta go," he said and scooted out of the booth.

Cliff grabbed his beer and stood. "Why? What's going on?"

"I'll tell you outside."

"Hey, you can't take that out of here," The bartender yelled at Cliff.

He smacked the bottle on the counter and followed Russell.

"Head over to the Medi-Clinic," Russell said as he fastened his seatbelt. "The one by the salon."

"Why? Is somebody hurt? Is it Deena? Estelle?"

Russell heard panic in his friend's voice. "No, nothing like that. The receptionist at the clinic recognized the guy in the picture. She says he's at the clinic now. We gotta talk to him before he leaves."

Cliff didn't say a word. He sped out of the parking lot toward the clinic.

"I'm going to call Deena and tell her what's happening." He dialed her number.

"You're not going to believe this," Russell said.

"You're not going to believe *this*," she replied.

Russell assumed the receptionist had called her, too. "You go first."

"Someone's been following me."

"What?" That's definitely not what he'd expected to hear.

"I tried to catch up with him, but I got stopped at a light and lost him. Or it could have been a *her*."

"Why would you stop at a light if you were trying to catch somebody?"

"Hello. It's the law."

Russell shook his head. "Did you get a license plate number at least?"

"No, but I know what kind of car it is. I think."

"Where are you now?"

"I'm headed back home. Where are you?"

Russell filled her in on the call from the receptionist and the mistake he made about thinking the guy they were looking for was Hispanic. She told him to stall and that she'd be there as quick as possible.

Russell hung up. Knowing those clinics, the guy would be there a while.

Chapter 16

Deena pulled up alongside Cliff's truck, and they all got out. She was anxious to see how similar this guy was to the picture Russell had drawn.

"How are we going to handle this?" Cliff asked as they stood in the parking lot. "Do we go in? Wait for him to come out? Do we need witnesses to what he says?"

"*We're* your witnesses," Russell said.

"We're also his friends." Deena looked around. Maybe she would get Kristy from the salon to be there. Then she remembered that it was Monday and the salon was closed. "Let's just talk to the guy first, and then we can call Guttman."

The two men followed her into the clinic.

When the receptionist spotted Russell, she smiled at him and pulled back the glass window. "Hi there, handsome. Glad you made it."

Deena rolled her eyes. How brazen of her. There were other people in earshot in the waiting room.

She followed Russell to the desk.

"I'm Gladys, by the way." She reached her bony hand through the window to shake Russell's. "*Glad is* how I feel seeing you again!" She giggled and batted her eyes.

Gag me, Deena thought. How many times had she used *that* line?

Gladys crooked her finger for Russell to lean in closer. "Mr. Pratt isn't one of our usuals. That's why I didn't recognize him when you showed me the picture. When he walked in to get his stitches removed today, I knew it was the man you were looking for and called you right away." She glared at Deena who was listening off to the side.

"We appreciate you calling," Russell said.

Lowering her voice even more, she said, "I'm not supposed to be telling you any of this, you know. Patient confidentiality and such. Would you all mind waiting outside and talking to him out there?"

"Not at all," Russell said and turned toward the door.

"And here's my number in case you need anything else." She slipped him a piece of paper.

Deena noticed that he reached to take it with his left hand, the one with his wedding ring on it.

The three of them made their way outside. It was still cold, so they sat in Deena's SUV to wait.

As soon as the man came out of the clinic door, they all got out of the car. It must have looked like a kidnapping. The man stepped back and put his hands up. "What's going on here?"

They all stopped except Cliff. "Uh, my name is Cliff. Do you remember me from last week?"

The man's eyes darted nervously between his three assailants. "I-I think so. Weren't you the guy putting that cooler in a car over there?" He pointed toward the salon.

Cliff dropped his head and let out a deep sigh. "Thank God."

Deena stepped up. "I know this sounds strange, but I'm an investigator." It wasn't actually a lie. She was investigating a murder. "A crime happened here last Monday, and you were a witness to Cliff's actions. Would you be willing to talk to the police?"

"Let me get this straight. I'm not being accused of anything, but this guy is?"

"That's right," Deena said. "All we need you to do is tell the police what happened when you helped Cliff that day."

He rubbed his chin. "I don't have a lot of time. I need to get back out to the ranch. If it won't take long, I'll do it."

"Thank you," they all said in unison.

Deena dialed Guttman's number. As she waited for him to come on the line, a white Cadillac with longhorns strapped to the hood pulled up. "Oh dear."

Guttman answered. She explained the situation, and he said he'd be right over. When she ended the call, Dan Carson was getting out of his car. "Well, how are my favorite murder suspects?" He grinned at Deena. "Anyone care to make a statement?"

"Not now, Dan. This is serious." Deena took his arm and tried to lead him back to his car.

He shook her hand loose and walked right up to the man on the sidewalk. "Dan Carson. I'm a reporter for the *Tribune*. Can I ask you a few questions?"

"Don't say anything," Deena said. She glared back at Dan. "I'll give you a statement."

His eyes widened. "On the record?"

"Yes, I'll tell you everything if you'll just give us a few minutes. Guttman is on his way, and if he sees you here, he might think we're up to something. A man's innocence is at stake."

Dan glanced at Cliff then back at Deena. "Okay, cutie. I'll wait back at Grady's."

He got in his Cadillac and drove off.

"Why do you think he followed us?" Russell asked.

"Think about it. I assume you went running out of the bar. He probably knew you had been at the police station for the line-up. His nose for news just told him something was up. I had forgotten he hangs out at Grady's."

They heard the siren blaring before they saw the police car. Guttman got out of the passenger's side. He walked up to the man. "You know this would be more comfortable back at the station."

"I don't have much time. I'm Harold Pratt." He shook hands with the detective.

Guttman pulled a piece of paper out of his pocket. It was the sketch Russell had made. "Looks more like Ramos than this guy." He glanced over at Russell who just shrugged.

"I'm going to record this interview, if that's all right with you." The uniformed officer who had driven the car handed him a small recorder.

"Fine with me. I've got nothing to hide."

Guttman turned to Deena. "Now if you will excuse us, I need to question this man in private."

"I've got something to tell you, too," Cliff said in a shaky voice. "It's about where I went after I left here Monday."

The detective shook his head. "Sounds like this case is about to get a lot more clear." He instructed Cliff to meet him back at the station and turned his attention back to Mr. Pratt.

Deena hugged Cliff and whispered in his ear, "The truth shall set you free."

* * *

WHEN SHE GOT IN HER car, she decided to call Betty to make sure they were still having class that night.

Nancy answered. "Betty's not here. She said she had to run some errands. As far as I know, there is still going to be class. That's what I've been telling everyone who's called."

Deena hung up. She would have to make her meeting with Dan. She wanted to get back in time to eat supper and to change into something more comfortable before going to the library for class.

Maybe she should call Gary. No, there was too much to try to explain over the phone. She wondered if Cliff had called Ian. It wouldn't be smart for Cliff to make a statement to the police without his attorney present. She dialed his number.

Just as she suspected, Cliff had not called him. "I'm meeting with another client," Ian said, "but I'll send Rob over there. We don't want Guttman to file perjury charges. I doubt he will since he has bigger fish to fry."

"Thanks. Hopefully, this will all be cleared up by the end of the day, and Cliff will no longer be a suspect."

"Well, yes. That very well may be the case."

She noticed something strange in Ian's voice. "What is it? You know something. Is it about Joseph Ramos?"

She waited two, three, four seconds.

At last Ian spoke. "There's been a new development. That's all I can say. I've got to go. I'll speak with you tomorrow."

Deena couldn't believe he hung up on her. Whatever he knew probably wasn't about Cliff; otherwise, he would have told her. He obviously had confidential information. She was glad he was so ethical since he was her attorney, too. It had to be about Ramos. Who else could it be?

As she drove to Grady's, she thought about what she'd say to Dan Carson. She actually wasn't that surprised he was asking her to go on the record. She'd have done the same thing if she were in his shoes. After all, he did tell her about Joseph Ramos.

It was time to pay the piper.

* * *

"YOU HAVE TO QUOTE ME as an anonymous source, you know," Deena told Dan as they sat in a back booth at Grady's.

Dan pulled a pen out of his shirt pocket. Apparently, he had forgotten to put the lid on it because there was a large black stain spreading out from the corner of his pocket. "It's a small town. A number of people will figure out who you are."

"That's fine. I just don't want to become a household name."

"So that brings me to my first question. How did you initially get involved in this case and how do you keep getting involved in Maycroft murder cases?"

"What? I'm not going to answer that."

"That wasn't for the newspaper. That was just for me." He laid the pen next to his glass of water.

"Oh. Well, in answer to the first part, Cliff is Russell's best friend. When Guttman first questioned him, I knew he didn't have a lawyer, so I called Ian."

Dan nodded his head as though that was a reasonable answer.

"As far as the other cases, being in the wrong place at the wrong time. Maybe?" She squeezed the lemon into her iced tea. "Why do you ask?"

"It seems to me that you have a knack for investigation, but when you had a chance at a job in that line of work, you quit after a week. Why?"

Deena took in a deep breath. It wasn't like this was the first time she'd contemplated that question. "I'm conflicted," she said. "On the one hand I really want to help people who are facing trouble, like my great-aunt when her son was discovered to have been murdered. On the other hand, I have a strong desire not to get killed. I'm not sure the two go together."

"I know what you mean. I've had a few close calls myself." He took a drink of water and crushed the ice with his teeth. "The difference between you and me is that you're connected. You have your husband and your brother. I'm pretty much alone."

"*Were* alone. Not anymore." She grinned. "Now you have Lydia."

"Slow done now. We're not booking a church yet or anything."

"She's a great girl, if I didn't mention it before. Her students love her, and she's easy to work with. You have my blessing to live happily ever after with her."

"Thanks, that means nothing to me."

"Oh, c'mon. You're getting too old to still be so cynical."

"What about my job?"

"What about it?"

"Do you want it?"

She wasn't quite sure what he was asking. "Do you mean, do I want to move somewhere and become a crime reporter?"

"No. I'm asking if you want to work for the *Tribune* and be the crime reporter."

She clasped her hands in front of her on the table. "Um, have you forgotten that I was fired as a reporter from the *Tribune*? Maybe you've noticed I haven't been around for the past six months."

"Here's the thing. Beazley is moving, and Lloyd wants me to be the assistant editor."

"Really? Congratulations!"

"But that means we're going to need a new crime reporter. Someone who knows their way around this town and isn't afraid to step on a few toes."

"Are you offering me a job? Does Lloyd Pryor know about this?"

"Yes, and he's one hundred percent on board. The change won't happen until the first of the year, so you can take a few weeks to think about it. Otherwise, we are going to have to start looking for someone from outside the area."

"Wow. Two whole weeks." She took a drink from her tea and watched the drops of water slide down the side of her glass. It had been raining those two weeks in March when she had helped Dan with the last murder investigation, and she had almost been killed. Was that something she really wanted to do again? What about her commitment to helping Sandra with the thrift store?

"I'll think about it." She dropped her hand on the table, signaling the end of that discussion.

"Okay," he said and picked up his pen. "Now tell me about your involvement with Joseph Ramos, Max Dekker's stalker."

She answered his questions, choosing her words carefully, knowing he would be quoting her in the newspaper. She much preferred being on the other side of the interview. After all, she always wanted to be an investigative reporter.

Chapter 17

Deena had just enough time to change clothes and eat a sandwich before heading off to the library for class.

The main part of the library was quiet and almost empty. A few people wandered the fiction stacks, and Nancy was helping an older man make copies. She could hear chatter coming from the reading room.

It looked like most of her fellow classmates were already there. She didn't see Lydia or Betty. She took her same seat in the back.

It's funny how people are such creatures of habit. As a teacher, she never had to assign seats in her class. Once a student sat somewhere they liked, that was their seat forever. Period. And you had better not try to sit there. Girls were the most protective. Seems like the same thing happened in church.

Max Dekker walked in a few minutes later, appearing understandably more haggard this week. His tie was slung over his shoulder and his jacket hung across his arm. He set his briefcase on the desk and opened it. As he peered inside, he straightened his tie and slipped on a blue version of the same jacket he had worn the week before.

He looked up and caught Deena staring at him. A smile crossed his face as he walked back to where she was sitting. "Mrs. Sharpe, may I have a word with you in private?"

All eyes followed them as they walked out of the back of the reading room. She swallowed hard, feeling like she'd just been hauled off to the principal's office.

"I just wanted to thank you for attending my wife's memorial on Saturday. Besides my realtor, you and your brother were the only local people there."

"Oh, you're welcome."

"We haven't made much of an effort to get involved in the town and haven't made any friends here. That will change. I hope I may consider you my friend."

"Of course." Guilt seeped into her mind, knowing she was hiding her ulterior motive for attending the service. She hoped it didn't show. It never hurt to be the teacher's pet.

"Detective Guttman told me what all you did in helping to identify Joseph Ramos and clear your friend of the crime. I must admit that I had my doubts about his story." He pulled a handkerchief from his pocket and used it to wipe his glasses. "The last thing I would ever want is to see an innocent man convicted of a crime he didn't commit."

"I agree. Cliff is a really good guy. He could never do something as horrible as this."

"Maybe I'll get to meet him and apologize in person for his...inconvenience."

Betty walked by carrying a plastic bag filled with cookies. Her face was flushed. "I'm just going to put these on the desk for you to take home," she said to Max without stopping.

Had she changed her mind about the two-timing cheater or was this gesture akin to giving an apple to the teacher? Deena turned her attention back to Max. "I heard they were going to be making an arrest soon. Joseph Ramos, I assume."

"That would be my guess, too, although I don't know for sure. He is one *seriously* troubled man." Max glanced at his watch. "Time to get started, I suppose." He motioned toward the door and followed Deena inside.

She took her seat just as Betty was coming back to their table. Deena did a quick head count. Only one person was absent. "Where's Lydia?" she whispered to Betty.

"After what happened the other day, she probably decided not to come back. I told you at least one person always drops out."

Max Dekker sat on the stool at the podium, looking professorial and distinguished. She was surprised he hadn't addressed the elephant in the room. Surely most people would expect him to say a word or two about his wife. "Last week we discussed characters. This week, we will be discussing plot."

Deena opened her spiral to the page where she had listed the suspects in Alexis Dekker's murder. She turned to a clean page.

"If you want to create a memorable, interesting plot, you really have to think outside the box. Surprise your readers," he said. "Don't make your villain too obvious."

A woman in the second row of tables raised her hand and waved it around like Horshack in *Welcome Back, Kotter*. "Ooh, ooh. I have a good idea. I'm going to write a mystery where an exterminator is a serial killer, and the story is told from the point of view of a rat!"

"Hmm." Max folded his arms across his chest. "That is definitely out-of-the-box thinking." He suppressed a grin and glanced back at Deena.

She smiled as he continued. Were they actually becoming friends? Could she be friends with someone like him? She hated to be judgmental, but the man was kissing his ex-wife the day after his current wife's murder. There had to be more to it. Maybe if she could get to know him better, he would give her the lowdown on the situation. Maybe he and his wife were separating. Maybe...

She tuned back in to the lecture.

"After you have come up with how the victim is killed, you need a list of suspects. Ask yourself, 'Who might have had a motive to kill?'"

Deena turned back a page in her spiral and looked at the list she had made previously. The first name listed was Max's. She drew a line through it. Even before today, she didn't believe he was a killer. She had looked in his eyes at the memorial and had gotten a sense about him. He didn't have an evil presence. She usually trusted her gut and was glad her instinct was right.

Next was Melissa. Besides Cliff, she was the last person to have seen Alexis alive. Sure, she might not have liked styling the woman's hair, but that was no motive for killing her. Guttman was probably right. Melissa had left town for a while because she was upset. Maybe she had a personal issue. Either way, she was in the clear. Deena drew a line through her name, too.

Cliff. She scratched his name out with several heavy lines. How could she have even suspected him of such a dastardly deed? The last name on the list was Guttman's. The dirty cop theory no longer made sense. It had been a longshot at best. She crossed out his name.

What about Harold Pratt, the man who had helped Cliff? Maybe he had a secret motive. If she were writing a book, he might be the perfect person to pin the murder on. But this was real life. He seemed like a nice guy who had stopped to do a good deed, and that's all. Besides, he had taken the time to talk to the detective on Cliff's behalf. She didn't bother adding his name to the list.

But there was another suspect. She added Joseph Ramos to her list. Max's voice buzzed in one side of her brain as he talked about means, motive, and opportunity. What about Ramos? She knew that Guttman would check his whereabouts for the time of the murder. That would be crucial to the case. He had already been accused of stalking Max Dekker. If he were in town, Ramos would certainly have a motive since he obviously blamed Max for the death of his wife. Even if that blame were misplaced, it would have been real to him.

Since Max had taken out a restraining order against Ramos, he was obviously a threat. That reminded her of something Dan said. Alexis had driven Max's car to the salon that evening. Had Ramos intended to kill Max instead? Or did he want to kill Max's wife so the writer would suffer just as he had? No wonder Max had described the man as troubled.

It was possible Ramos only showed up after he heard about Alexis's murder, but if that was the case, it left the big question still unanswered. Who killed Alexis Dekker? Was there another suspect out there? One who hadn't yet shown his—or her—true colors?

A noise in the back of the room made Deena glance over her shoulder. The reading room door opened and in walked Linus Guttman with three uniformed policemen at his heels. They walked straight up to the podium. "Maxwell Dekker, you are under arrest for the murder of Alexis Dekker."

One officer put his hand on Max's arm while the other clapped on the handcuffs. Silence fell over the room. The third officer pulled on latex gloves and began putting Max's belongings back in his briefcase. He picked up the case and led Max toward the exit.

Guttman continued. "You have the right to remain silent. You have the right to an attorney. If you do not have an attorney..."

* * *

IT WAS LIKE DÉJÀ VU, only this time Betty wasn't the first to speak.

"Who do you suppose we call to get our money back for this class?" It was the exterminator-plot lady.

Several people around her shook their heads.

"I'll call and see what I can find out," Betty said. Her voice shook more this time. "Before you leave, please take some cookies from the office. I bought enough for everyone." She stood next to the wall and wrung her hands as everyone filed out. "Deena, wait up."

When everyone else had left, she walked over to the table to pick up her notepad. "Did you know this was going to happen?"

"No. Why would you think I'd have known?"

"Because you've been...involved...investigating...something like that."

Deena resisted the urge to roll her eyes. Good ol' Maycroft grapevine at play again. "I'm just as surprised as you are. In fact, I thought they were going to arrest a different suspect. Someone who had a beef about one of Max's books."

"His books? What's that about?"

Deena considered telling her about Joseph Ramos, but if she did, she would be as big a gossip as the rest of the leaves on the grapevine. Besides, it wasn't like she and Betty were good friends, as she once believed. "I bet there's going to be a story all about it in tomorrow's newspaper. You can read all about it then." She put her satchel on her shoulder and headed toward the door.

"Let me walk you out at least."

"It's actually still a little light out. I'll be fine."

"No bother. I feel a little responsible for you being in this mess since I talked you into taking the class in the first place."

Deena couldn't muster the energy to argue with Betty. She seemed so anxious to make amends. But the wind had just been totally knocked out of Deena's sails. Could she have really been so wrong in her estimation of Max Dekker? Could her gut instinct have failed her so badly? Her head was pounding and spinning at the same time.

They walked around to the back of the lot where Deena had parked. It was dusk, but the front lights in the parking lot had come on and the Fitzhugh Library glowed like a football stadium on a Friday night.

Deena didn't want to tell Betty about Cliff and how she probably would have gotten involved in spite of taking the class. Still, she wouldn't have fallen for those puppy dog eyes of Max Dekker if she hadn't taken the class. "You're right. I would have been elbow deep in batter instead of blood."

Betty frowned.

"Sorry. The teacher in me went for the alliteration." She used the button on her key fob to unlock the car door.

Betty sniffed the air. "Do you smell something?" She looked like one of those drug-sniffing dogs inspecting the school lockers. She walked around to the other side of the car and bent down. "There's something pooling under your car."

Deena bent down and saw a puddle shining on the pavement. She pulled out her phone and turned on the flashlight feature. "Holy moly. What is that?"

"Pop your hood and we'll look." Betty moved to the front of the car.

"I don't know how. I'll just drive home and let Gary take a look at it."

Betty tilted her head. "Maybe you should sign up for a car maintenance class instead of cooking. There should be a handle to pull on the left side down near the floorboard."

Deena used her flashlight and pulled on a handle she had never noticed before.

The hood clicked, and Betty raised it up.

Deena walked to the front to shine the light around for Betty. "What are we looking for?"

Betty leaned in closer. "It looks like your brake line is leaking."

* * *

DEENA CLUTCHED THE edge of the car to steady herself. What on earth was going on? Had someone cut her brake line? Who would do this?

Her first instinct was to call Gary. Instead, she dialed 9-1-1.

By this time, a small crowd who had mingled in the parking lot after class had gathered around. Between bites of cookies, they mumbled their speculations about what might have happened.

After explaining her emergency, she called Gary. She could hear Hurley barking in the background and assured him that the police were on their way. He had a million questions, but she just told him to come get her and she would give him the details then.

Betty had joined the onlookers. They stood off to the side almost as if they were afraid to get too close in fear of catching some deadly virus. Deena wasn't sure what to do. She stood by the car. Obviously, she didn't want to get in, just in case the police wanted to dust it for fingerprints. Did they still do that, or was that just something they did on TV?

The squeal of sirens cut through the night air and was a welcome relief. Two squad cars pulled up, and three officers emerged. Deena recognized one as Cassidy Nelson.

"Officer—I mean, Sergeant Nelson. Thanks for coming."

"When I heard your name, I decided to come myself." She pulled out her notepad. "So tell me what happened here."

"I was in the library for class—a writing class—with Max Dekker."

Sergeant Nelson raised an eyebrow.

"When I came out to my car, my friend Betty smelled something." Deena looked around for Betty who was standing at the back of the crowd. "I opened the hood, and Betty said my brake line had been cut. After what happened to Alexis Dekker..."

"I understand." She walked over to where one of the officers was looking under the hood with a flashlight.

Deena spotted Gary's red Mercedes pulling into the parking lot. He parked and jumped out of the car. He looked over at the officers and said, "Here we go again."

"Except this time, I'm the victim." The words made her quiver.

Sergeant Nelson walked over to get a statement from Betty. Another officer asked if anyone in the crowd had seen anything suspicious. The third officer snapped pictures of the car and the engine.

"I'm glad you're okay," Gary said, wrapping her up in a bear hug. "If Betty hadn't seen that..."

"I know." As she looked over Gary's shoulder, something caught her eye. A white Ford sedan was parked next to the back of the building. Her mouth dropped open, and she stepped back out of Gary's grasp. She started toward the car. Was someone in it? Was someone watching her?

"Deena?" Gary called out.

As she got closer, she could tell the car was empty. She turned around to answer him, and there, on the next row of the lot, was another white Ford sedan—also unoccupied.

Gary caught up with her. "What is it, hon?"

She felt her mouth move but her voice seemed to come from a distance. "Those cars. Someone has been following me. A white Ford."

Gary led her back toward the police cars. "Officer Nelson."

"Sergeant," Deena corrected him.

"I'm going to take her inside to sit down," Gary said.

"I'll be right in," Sergeant Nelson said. "Get her some water."

Inside, the library was, well, as quiet as a library. She let Gary lead her to the first table they came to.

Nancy rushed up. "What's going on outside, Deena? I saw the police cars. Did someone try to mug you?"

"Can you get her a glass of water?" Gary asked, his face pale with worry.

Nancy nodded and headed toward the office.

He sat next to Deena. "Why didn't you tell me someone had been following you?" There was an edge to his voice.

"I didn't know if I was just imagining it. Now I think it was true."

"Did you see the car? Get the license number?"

"No. It was a white Ford sedan. There are two in the parking lot."

Nancy returned with a cup of water and two of Betty's cookies. "Here." She set them on the table in front of Deena.

Gary gave Nancy a quick synopsis of the incident.

Deena tried to regain her senses, and her fear subsided. She clenched her teeth and breathed faster. "As soon as I find out who did this, I'm gonna strangle them!"

Gary and Nancy both stared at her, wide-eyed expressions on their faces.

She turned to Nancy. "Do you know anyone around here who drives a white Ford sedan?"

"Sure," Nancy said. "Betty does."

*　*　*

"WE'RE GOING TO HAVE to impound your car," Sergeant Nelson said to Deena. "We'll see if we can get any evidence off of it. I have a truck on the way to pick it up." She turned to Nancy. "The library is closed, as of now. Will you make sure no one comes in besides my officers?"

"Yes, ma'am," Nancy said and headed for guard duty by the front entrance.

The sergeant pulled a chair up next to Deena. "I need to ask you some more questions."

"First, I need to tell you something." Deena sucked in a calming breath and let it out slowly. "For the last week, I've had the sense that someone was following me. I kept seeing the same white Ford sedan. First at the police station and then on the street several times. I never saw the driver."

"That's a pretty common vehicle around here. Did you get a license number?"

"No. But just now, I saw there were two of them parked out back. Apparently one belongs to Betty Donaldson, but I don't know who owns the other."

"Hmm. Let me get an officer on it. Hopefully, the cars are still out there." She hurried outside.

"What do you think?" Deena asked, watching her husband's face. The laugh lines seemed deeper than she remembered.

"Well, obviously it wasn't Betty. She just...she just saved your life."

Deena rubbed her face with both hands. "That's right. If she hadn't seen that puddle..."

"The police can track down the driver of the other car—and every white Ford sedan in Maycroft, if that's what it takes."

Betty came flying in through the back door of the library. "Deena, I'm so glad you are okay."

Deena stood and threw her arms around Betty. She could feel the woman tense up, but Deena didn't care. She squeezed even harder. "Thank you. You saved my life."

Betty wrangled herself free. "I can't believe this happened. Who would want to kill you?"

"That's the million dollar question," Gary said. "Hopefully, the police can find out."

Deena sat back down and put her hand on Gary's leg. It was comforting to have him near her, like her own private security blanket. "It has to be related to the Dekker case, don't you think?"

Betty just stared and shook her head. "I have no idea."

Nancy opened the door for Sergeant Nelson.

As usual, the look on her face was blank, a real asset for a law enforcement officer. "We ran the plates on the two cars. One is registered to Phillip Donaldson."

"That's my husband," Betty said. "What's this about?"

"The other is a rental car. According to the car company, it was rented by Max Dekker."

Chapter 18

Anger still clouded her thoughts when she woke up Tuesday to say good-bye to Gary. She had to "cross her heart and hope to die" before she could get him to let her stay alone at the house. Of course with no car, there wasn't much she could do anyway.

She had lain awake for at least an hour the night before wondering who could have wanted her dead. Sure, she had ruffled some feathers in town in the past but not enough to warrant this kind of revenge. Besides, the timing was too coincidental. It simply had to be related to the Dekker case.

Max Dekker. If the police thought he killed his wife, maybe they would find evidence that he tried to kill her, too. But why would he? He went out of his way to thank her. That didn't seem like the action of a killer. Plus, it probably happened at the library. Wouldn't that be too obvious if he were already under suspicion? In her opinion, Max was innocent on both counts. Still, she couldn't dismiss the fact that he had the means and opportunity to do it.

Another thought crossed her mind. Maybe she and Alexis Dekker had been random victims of a serial killer. The thought made her stomach turn. Which was worse: being someone's specific target or having a madman on the loose in their small, cozy community?

She stared at the ceiling wondering what she should do. She would call Russell later. It would upset him if he heard about her situation secondhand. News traveled faster than a roadrunner in Maycroft.

She remembered that Dan's article about Max Dekker's arrest would be in today's newspaper. She hopped out of bed and hurried to the front door and grabbed the newspaper off the front porch. The *Northeast Texas Tribune* had recently increased their circulation to five days a week. They didn't publish on Saturday and Sunday since so many people in their region got their weekend news from the Dallas newspaper.

She poured herself a cup of coffee, still warm from Gary's morning brew and sat at the kitchen table. The headline read: "Local Author Arrested for Murder." Apparently, Dan had a late night revising the headline and updating the story to make today's edition.

She read the article carefully, seeing if there were any new details. Guttman was quoted as saying he wouldn't release any new information until the suspect had retained counsel. Ian had told her there had been a new development. She was hoping something in the article explained why the evidence pointed to Max Dekker and not Joseph Ramos.

Interesting. Who would Max get to represent him? Surely not anyone from around here. He likely had a bevy of lawyers on retainer in New York.

The bing-bong of the doorbell made her jump, causing Hurley to go into a barking frenzy. She glanced out the front window but didn't see a car. She looked through the peephole expecting to see a neighbor—just not this one.

"Mr. Cooper." Luckily, she caught herself before calling him Mr. Creeper. "What can I do for you?"

"It's not what you can do for me; it's what I can do for you."

Ugh. The last thing she needed was for Peeping Tom to paraphrase JFK. She stepped out onto the porch to keep from inviting him inside. Her foot still throbbed. She folded her arms and stared.

"You see, I keep my eye on the neighborhood."

Duh. We see you staring at us through the fence all the time.

"I'm not *officially* a member of the Neighborhood Watch, but I do what I can to keep our neighborhood safe."

"Uh-huh."

"Well, for the past few days, I noticed a strange car driving slowly down our street. I wouldn't have thought much about it, except it seemed to slow down in front of your house."

Goosebumps rose up on her arms. "What did it look like? Did you see the driver?"

"No, no. It was always dark. I didn't see the driver. Whenever I went to get my binoculars—let's just say it was too far away."

"But you saw the car. What did it look like?"

"Wouldn't you rather have this conversation inside? I have a pot of coffee ready at the house."

"No, thanks. But this is important. Can you tell me about the car?"

"Very well, then. It was white. A four-door sedan. Nothing special or unusual about it."

"And you said you saw it drive past after dark? Did you see it last night?"

"No, not since Sunday. But since this whole murder business has popped up, I thought you could never be too safe. A pretty woman like you needs to—"

"Thank you, Mr. Cooper. I need to make a few calls. Nice seeing you."

She stepped inside and closed the door. Hurley looked up with his brown eyes asking for an update. "Nobody special," she said, and he trotted back into the den.

Who should she call first? Gary or Guttman? Maybe Sergeant Nelson. She decided against calling Gary since the information was non-specific. He would be surprised, though, to learn that Edwin Cooper had had the nerve to come to their front door.

She decided to call Sergeant Nelson. Deena knew her and trusted her more than Guttman. Plus, she and Gary had talked to her previously about their creepy neighbor. She would know who he was.

The receptionist put Deena's call right through. She quickly explained the information she had received from Edwin Cooper. What Sergeant Nelson said next was a complete surprise. She hung up the phone after agreeing to come down to the station to make a statement. They were sending a squad car to pick her up.

Should she call Ian? Did she need her attorney to go with her? As she walked in a daze back to the bedroom to get dressed, she repeated the sergeant's words in her head. *Your case has been turned over to Detective Guttman as part of the Dekker investigation.*

Chapter 19

"Thanks for coming down, Mrs. Sharpe." Detective Guttman's tie was loose, and his suit looked like he'd slept in it. "I need to ask you a few questions about last night." He fumbled with a stack of folders on his desk.

Deena wriggled in the faux leather chair across from him. She looked down at her feet and noticed she was wearing two different shoes. Both were ballet flats, but one was black and the other was navy blue. This wasn't the first time she'd left the house with mismatched shoes. It was more common, though, back in her teaching days. She couldn't believe how much her life had changed in just a year.

"Tell me when you first noticed brake fluid under your car?"

"It was at the library last night. Actually, my friend Betty noticed it."

"Where had your car been parked prior to that?"

"In my garage. In case you're wondering, my husband checked the floor of the garage and driveway. There was no fluid in either place."

He made a note. "When did you first notice a white car following you? Sergeant Nelson reported that you stated it was a Ford sedan. Do you know the model?"

"No. They all look about the same to me. It seems like the first time I saw it was when I was here talking to you on Saturday. It was parked in the back of the lot. Someone was sitting in it, but I couldn't see who it was."

Guttman made a note. "I'll get security to check out the video and see if they can get a plate number. When else?"

"I saw it again on Sunday driving back from the Pit Stop Café out on the highway."

"Are you sure it was the same car? White Fords are pretty common."

"Obviously, I can't be sure, but my gut told me it was. People say I have pretty good instincts about this sort of thing."

"Like how you thought Max Dekker was innocent of murder?"

Ouch. "Low blow. I don't have all the evidence you guys have. I still find it hard to believe he killed his wife. And what about Joseph Ramos?

"We'll get to that in a minute. Back to the car."

"I saw it again on Monday and tried to follow it. Unfortunately, it got away."

"You still didn't see the driver or model?"

"Nope." She looked down at her shoes. So much for her attention to detail. "Oh, I remember something else. Last week when I was leaving Ian Davis's office to come here, I heard a car speed off. I didn't see it, but it seemed suspicious."

Guttman looked at his notes. "That would have been on Wednesday, correct?"

"Yes. Why does all this matter? Do you think Max Dekker was following me and tried to kill me?"

Guttman closed the folder and laid his hands on the desk. "I'm going to tell you something in confidence. Sergeant Nelson said you helped out on a previous case and could be trusted."

Deena's heart beat a little faster. "I can be." She stopped herself from making the pinky swear she used to do with Russell.

"As you may know, sometimes law enforcement will keep some details of a crime out of the news as a strategic move. We did that in this case."

Deena slid forward on her seat.

"Melissa Engels, the hairdresser at the beauty shop, reported seeing a white Ford in the parking lot while Mrs. Dekker was there. It was before Cliff Abel showed up with the cooler."

Deena's mind traveled back to that day. "Could it have belonged to the man who helped Cliff?"

"Mr. Pratt? No. We checked him out."

"Maybe Max Dekker just stopped by to say hello before going to the library."

"Melissa said he did not come in."

"Is that why Melissa took off?"

"She was afraid someone would think she was a snitch. Apparently, she had had some trouble in the past and didn't want to get involved. We are trying to track her down so that she can testify for us at trial."

Deena sat back and fiddled with her purse. "Did you know that he had rented the Ford?"

"Yes. He got it for his wife to drive a few weeks back since they only had one car when they moved here. Apparently, though, she preferred his car. You see, we have been following a lot of different leads, but Max Dekker has been our prime suspect all along."

Deena could feel her muscles tense. "So what was his motive for following me and then trying to kill me?"

"This is only speculation, of course, but you saw him with his ex-wife the day after the murder. You brought your evidence to the police. You continued trying to help clear Cliff Abel of the crime. In short, you were getting in the way of finding another suspect."

"So what about Joseph Ramos? He was here in town for the memorial. That's a fact. Did he have an alibi for the time of the murder?"

"Yes. Not as solid as we had hoped, but we are still investigating it."

Deena didn't want to accept the fact that Max was guilty. She took one last stab at it. "Have you considered that there could be a serial killer on the loose cutting random people's brake lines?"

Guttman leaned back in his chair. "Mrs. Sharpe, there's more. I'm sure Ian Davis told you about the handkerchief."

"What? No."

"Mr. Davis said you found a greasy handkerchief among Mrs. Dekker's clothes at the thrift shop. When his wife, Sandra, told him about it, he called me. I had it tested. Yesterday it came back positive for brake fluid."

Deena put her hand to her mouth as she gasped. That must have been the new information Ian had mentioned to her.

"Mrs. Sharpe, you're a bright woman. Didn't you find it strange that Mr. Dekker would donate a box of his wife's clothes to the thrift shop so soon after his wife's death? He probably didn't realize her name was sewn into some of the garments."

"But this is all circumstantial evidence."

"True, but the District Attorney thought it was enough for a trial."

"I can't believe it. I mean, I can—but I can't."

He shook his head. "Sometimes good people do bad things."

Deena sat back in her chair. "So you really think he tried to kill me, too?"

"There's one more piece of evidence we have found so far. Last night when we took Mr. Dekker into custody, we found another greasy handkerchief in his briefcase. It's at the lab. We expect it to come back positive for brake fluid."

Deena's cell phone rang. She answered it without thinking. The man on the other end of the line sounded nervous. When he said his name, Deena recognized it as belonging to a senior partner of the law firm of Lyons and Sons. "My client, Max Dekker, would very much like to speak to you," he said.

"Me?" She was shocked.

"Yes. He is currently being held in the Perry County Jail and is not scheduled to be released until later this evening. If you could go over there, we would greatly appreciate it."

Deena was conflicted, but her curiosity won out. "I'll be there shortly." She looked at the detective. "Seems that Max Dekker wants to talk to me."

Guttman tilted his head. "Interesting. That's your choice, of course, but realize that everything you say will be recorded."

"I know. Is this going to be a problem?"

"Not at all. I trust you not to bring up Melissa Engels's testimony about seeing his car."

"*A* car," she said. "We don't know yet if it is his. What about the other evidence? Does he know about it? Can I question him about that?"

"Absolutely. We've already interviewed him about the other information. I'm not expecting a jailhouse confession, but maybe his explanation will help our case. Especially if he changes his story down the road."

"Have you finished with my car?"

"Ah, yes. That's another matter I wanted to ask you about." He flipped through a few pages in the folder. "Were you aware that there was a GPS tracking device mounted to the underside of your car?"

* * *

THERE WAS NO GETTING around it. Reality hit her like a Mack truck. It hadn't been her imagination. She wasn't the victim of a random act of violence. Someone had targeted her and wanted her dead, and the most likely suspect was Max Dekker. That realization made her head spin and her stomach lurch.

She wasn't used to the feeling of having enemies. Sure, she had been in danger before—usually as a result of getting herself in a pickle.

Thank goodness for Betty or else she would have been the next headline in the newspaper. She tried to shake the maudlin thoughts from her head and looked around to see if anyone had been reading her mind. The other patrons in the reception area of the police station were either glued to their cell phones or staring helplessly into space.

Where were they with her car? This was worse than waiting for her name to be called at the DMV. Worse than waiting for the lines to move at the bank's drive-through. Worse than waiting for the biopsy results from her doctor.

Actually, that had been worse. A lot worse. *Focus.*

What would she say to Max Dekker when she got over to the jail? He had scheduled the meeting, so she should let him do all the talking. Would he deny everything? Probably. Would she believe him? Why should she?

A man wearing a brown jumpsuit walked into the waiting area holding a clipboard. "Deena Sharpe," he called out.

"Here," she said and stood.

He walked up and shoved a pen at her. "Sign here for your car. We'll send you a bill for fixing your brake line."

She obeyed and took her car keys from him. "Super."

Walking out to her car, she squeezed the keychain like a talisman. She relished the familiarity and comfort it gave her by just holding it in her hand. Once inside her car, she let out a deep sigh. She felt safe.

The sun's rays pouring through the glass illuminated a spot on the steering wheel. A smudge of fingerprint powder missed in the clean up stared back at her, a stark reminder that things were not exactly as they were before. Perhaps they never would be. She shuddered as if a cold wind had passed through her. This must have been what experts called "victim mentality."

She refused to give in to that kind of thinking. It wasn't as if the whole world was after her; it was just one person. As long as he was locked up, she would be safe. She started the engine, and the air conditioning blew dust all around. She imagined the specs to be tiny angels watching over her.

Pulling out of the parking lot and turning toward the jail, she knew one question she would be asking Max Dekker for sure. *Why did you want to kill me?*

Chapter 20

The room where inmates spoke with visitors looked like something out of a 1990s crime drama. Maycroft hadn't updated to a video monitor system of communicating with visitors. All three of the visitor cubicles were filled.

There was another woman waiting along with her. She was middle-aged and busied herself with knitting. She must be a regular. Was she there to see her child or husband? Maybe it was her brother. Had her brother gotten caught writing bad checks? Maybe it was a DUI. He could be an alcoholic. Or on drugs.

An officer appeared and called the woman's name. She smiled and made her way to the now-open cubicle. Deena leaned over to try to see who the woman was talking to. She leaned out a little too far and the folding chair skidded out from under her, causing her to crash onto the hard linoleum floor. Everyone turned to look as she quickly picked herself up and righted the chair. She scooped up the contents of her handbag.

Subtle, Deena.

It was her turn. She sat down as Max Dekker shuffled his way into the chair on the other side of the Plexiglas window.

He gave her what she assumed to be a grateful smile. Even in an orange jumpsuit, the man looked distinguished.

She waited for him to pick up the phone before putting the receiver to her ear.

"Thank you for coming."

She nodded, realizing her jaw was clenched tight.

"You know, it's kind of interesting in here. I'm getting lots of background research for my next book." He waited for her to respond.

Nothing.

"The food isn't too bad if you like scrambled eggs made out of cardboard." Another pause. "Do you realize there are actually people living in the civilized world who have no familiarity with deodorant? Who would have guessed?"

"I thought you were retired," Deena said flatly.

"A writer's gotta write, ya know. Can't sit around with my boots up jest sewin' cott'n and checkin' the trot lines."

Deena's face kept its steady composure, but she was a little surprised. It was the first time she'd heard Max break out of his sophisticated New York accent and get back to his Southern roots.

"Well, enough chitchat," he said. "I suppose you are wondering why I asked to see you."

She blinked her eyes, trying to keep her vow to let him do the talking.

"I assume you know the circumstances behind my arrest. According to my attorney, they may be adding on an attempted murder charge as well."

He paused, but she refused to gift him a reaction.

"None of it is true. I didn't do it. I never killed my wife or tried to kill you. Now, I realize that you probably expected me to say that, and I've been trying to come up with a way to convince you—and everyone else—that I'm telling the truth. The problem is that I haven't been able to."

She lifted an eyebrow. That was unexpected. "What do you want from me Mr. Dekker?"

"I want your help. I've written enough mysteries to know that I need someone from the area who knows the people here to help prove my case."

"What about your lawyer? He's from Maycroft."

"He's temporary. My New York attorney only does contracts, so he recommended a hotshot criminal defense lawyer from Houston. He's arriving tomorrow. Even he will need someone who knows the people here to help him. From what I've seen and heard, you're a pretty sharp investigator—no pun intended."

She shook her head. "Why should I help you? How do you know I don't think you're guilty?"

Max rubbed the side of his face slowly with his hand.

Was that the hand of a killer? The same hand that had crafted all those wonderful stories?

"Last week when we first met, you challenged me. I recognized right away that you had gumption. You want to know the truth behind this case as much as I do. I can see it in your eyes."

She blinked and looked away. He may not be innocent, but he was definitely perceptive. She looked back at him. "If not you, then who?"

"That's what we need to find out. Someone is framing me. Someone put those oily handkerchiefs in my briefcase. Someone took that box of clothes to the thrift store. Someone killed my wife and tried to kill you. We need to find out who it was."

The guard standing behind Max looked at his watch and gave her the wrap-it-up sign by twirling his fingers. She looked back at Max whose attention was fixed on something behind her. She turned just as Max's ex-wife, Barbara Conroy, raced up and grabbed the receiver out of Deena's hand.

She shouted into the phone. "You lying snake! How could you change your will and leave me out of it. Charity? You're leaving it all to some charity? I haven't hung around all these years to wind up alone and penniless." She shot an angry look at Deena before turning back to Max. "And, who in the blazes is Lizzie Bogmire?"

* * *

AFTER THE OFFICERS restrained Barbara Conroy and hauled her away, there was nothing more for Deena to do except go home and sort out what had happened. She sat on her patio watching Hurley sniff and chase the fall leaves that danced around the grass, forming a colorful blanket on the rippling water of the pool. She hugged her knees and pulled the sweater tighter around her.

Max Dekker was telling the truth, she was sure of it. As for his relationship with Barbara Conroy, she was stumped. If he had wanted to be with his ex-wife, why didn't he just file for divorce from Alexis? Or better yet, why did he re-marry her? One thing she knew was that Max Dekker was more fickle than a love-struck teenager.

Barbara showed her true colors when she asked those questions about Max's will. Seemed like she was in it more for the money than anything else. If it turned out that Max truly loved her, he must be devastated right now, especially if he killed Alexis to be with her.

No, that didn't happen. She rested her chin on her knees. Could it have been the other way around? Could Barbara have wanted to get rid of Alexis to get back with Max? *Sounds reasonable.* Maybe Barbara dropped the box of clothes off at the back of the thrift shop. That would make sense. Out with the old, in with the new.

But was she in town when Alexis was murdered? Max's attorney would likely offer her up as a suspect and force Detective Guttman to check her alibi. Even if she had an alibi, her behavior might lead to reasonable doubt.

So if Barbara killed Alexis, was she the person who cut Deena's brake line? Greed may have made her want Alexis dead so she could get her hands on Max's money, but Deena wasn't worth anything to her dead.

The only other motives she could come up with were jealousy and self-protection. Deena hadn't done anything to make the woman jealous except show up at the memorial. Could Barbara have seen Deena as a threat? Maybe Deena was getting too close to the truth. Maybe Barbara was the person following her in Max's rental car.

If Deena wasn't in deep enough already, she was about six feet under now. She had witnessed Barbara's outburst at the jail, so Guttman would need to interview her. There would be a deposition. Obviously, she should let Ian know what was going on.

Not yet though. She knew that as her lawyer, he would advise her to stay away from Max Dekker and the entire case. That would be wise of her to do. But sometimes doing the dumb thing gets the best results. She wanted to talk to Max and ask him a few more questions. He would be out on bond tomorrow. Maybe she would go see him.

She needed to work out one last detail. It was the last thing Barbara said. She had asked Max about Lizzie Bogmire. How on earth would Max Dekker have anything to do with Betty's sister?

Chapter 21

Deena walked up to the front door of the Dekker house. There were several cars parked out front, none of which were a white Ford sedan. Max's rental car was likely still at the police impound. She knocked and waited.

Last night she had told Gary everything that happened with the exception of her plans to talk to Max one last time. Not telling him wasn't a lie, but it was still a deception. She knew Max's attorneys would be present, so she would be safe. Once she had her questions answered, she would go see Ian and tell him everything she knew—just like she'd promised Gary.

A man wearing a blue suit and thick horned-rimmed glasses opened the door. Surely, this wasn't the high-priced defense attorney from Houston. It had been her experience that the better looking an attorney was, the more successful he or she tended to be. Juries liked attractive lawyers.

"You must be Mrs. Sharpe," the man said. "Come in."

She followed him back to the den. It looked exactly as she would expect to see in a writer's house. One entire wall was covered in bookshelves and filled to the brim with hardbacks and paperbacks and knick-knacks of every sort. The books were not arranged in any particular order from what she could see, unlike the ones at Betty's house, but instead were shoved into every nook and cranny like treasures among treasures.

Max was sitting on the sofa with a notepad in his lap. She could see an ankle monitor around his leg where his pant leg was hiked up. Obviously, he was under strict surveillance, as the rich often are. Unlike regular folks, the rich have the means and resources to disappear.

He stood and greeted her. "Mrs. Sharpe. Glad you decided to come by. This is David Callahan, my attorney, and this is..."

The man with glasses introduced himself and the pretty paralegal sitting at the kitchen table typing away on a laptop.

"Nice to meet you all," Deena said.

Callahan walked over and gave her a two-handed shake, covering the top of her hand with his. It was the kind of warm handshake you give when greeting an old friend or a distant relative. "I'm delighted to meet you. I think you are going to be a real key to this case and to ensuring that justice is served." His deep blue eyes locked on to hers.

She took a seat across from the sofa.

David Callahan looked like he'd stepped out of the pages of *GQ* magazine. He was probably middle-aged, but had a boyish face and a dimpled chin. His deep tan was likely a spray-on job, but looked as natural as if he'd spent all his time on the beach. Even his dark hair had that messy but perfectly styled look you see on movie stars. Only thing missing was the perpetual five o'clock shadow.

"I understand you were at the jail talking to Mr. Dekker when Ms. Conroy arrived," Callahan said.

If sound had a texture, Callahan's voice would be velvet. She wanted to hear more.

When Deena didn't respond, he continued. "We feel like Mrs. Conroy could be responsible for the death of Alexis Dekker and the attempt on your life as well."

Those words brought her back from dreamland. She probably needed a lawyer here. She was way out of her league with this guy. Good-looking or not, he was still an attorney and had his own agenda.

"I—I really didn't come here to answer your questions, Mr. Callahan. I came here to get answers of my own."

"Call me David, please," he said as glances shot around the room.

Max, however, looked directly at her. "I understand," he said. "Ask me anything you want. I'm an open book."

"Ha! Good one," ol' blue eyes said. "Make a note of that. We'll use it at trial."

Max shot an annoyed look at his attorney and then re-focused on Deena.

"I'd rather speak to you in private, if possible." She hadn't planned to say that, but the audience gathered had made her uncomfortable.

"You've heard of attorney-client privilege, I'm sure," Callahan said. "You are free to speak here."

"That would apply if you were *my* attorney, Mr. Callahan, but you're not." She turned back to Max. "It's about Lizzie Bogmire."

Max's eyebrows shot up. He pushed back the gray hair at his temple. "Gentlemen—and lady—will you excuse us for a few minutes." He stood and motioned for Deena to follow him.

They stepped out onto the back patio with a row of Adirondack chairs looking out into the pasture. After they sat, Max began talking slowly, as if choosing each word with perfect care. "I've always been a story-teller, you know, ever since I was a child. It's both my passion and my nemesis. I'm going to tell you something I'm not proud of. Something I've only ever told one person in my life, and now she's dead."

Deena's body stiffened and her eyes grew large.

"Oh, don't worry. Nothing's going to happen to you. It just seems like 'the jig is up,' as they say, and it's time to come clean. Before long everyone will know the story, and everyone will know that Max Dekker is a liar and a thief."

Deena's throat felt like a withered-up cactus in the dry Texas heat. She tried to swallow and then managed to croak out a question. "What does this have to do with Lizzie Bogmire?"

He blinked his eyes and gave her a crooked smile, resting his head in the chair as though he were taking a trip a thousand miles away. "You see, back when I was young and reckless, I thought I knew everything—especially about writing. After all, I was a young professor on the tenure track at the university teaching creative writing. If my alma mater thought I knew what I was talking about, then I must. Right?

"Well, no one had told that to the New York publishing houses. I couldn't even get an agent, much less a book deal. I could have wallpapered my little house in Austin with all the rejection letters I had received. Depressing. I was the consummate tortured artist. This went on for several years. My hopes and dreams seemed to be crashing down all around me.

"Then I met Alexis. She was one of the agents to whom I had sent my manuscript. She said it wasn't very good but thought it had potential. She asked if I had anything else, perhaps something better. I didn't. However, I had just read a short story by one of my college students. It was powerful. It was impressive. It was in my file cabinet drawer."

Deena leaned in a little closer. Was this story going where she thought it was going?

"If you're thinking I sent a copy of it off to Alexis, you'd be right. She loved it. She encouraged me to come to New York to work with an editor friend of hers. I took off a semester from the university and finished the novel. We changed the title to *Crimson Waters*. A publishing house picked it up, and it became a bestseller. The rest, as they say, is history."

"And Lizzie Bogmire?"

"She was very young and a little naive. She was the gal who wrote the short story. I gave her a B."

"So when the novel came out, did you ever hear from her? Did she find out what you did?"

"Back in those days, manuscripts were typed. On typewriters."

"I remember."

"Unless you typed with carbon paper, that one copy was all you had. I had the only copy of the story. Some six years after the release, she called me up. Threatened to sue me. I told her she had no proof. I was such a jerk back then. So full of myself. I told her to give me her address, and I'd send her something." He shook his head. "You know what I did? I sent her a signed copy of the book."

"Tacky. Really tacky."

"That was the last time I heard from Lizzie Bogmire, but believe me, it wasn't the last time I thought about her. The older I get, the more guilt I have."

"What about all of your other books? Did you write those?"

"Yes, indeed. Turns out, I was a pretty good storyteller after all. Just needed a little spit and polish from some of New York's finest editors. Just like Alexis thought."

Deena stared at a pair of squirrels jumping from branch to branch, and thought about how simple life could be for earth's non-human inhabitants. "You said I was the second person you told this story to. I assume Alexis was the first."

"Yes, and that was the beginning of my undoing. As my agent, the person who started my meteoric rise to fame in the book world, I was indebted to her. Unfortunately, I confused gratitude with love. We married six weeks to the day my book hit the bestseller list. Of course, it didn't hurt that she had wavy blonde hair and mile-long legs that would keep most men awake at night." His melancholy smile matched his tone.

"But once the passion wore off, there wasn't much left. Then I met Barbara. She was a paralegal at my lawyer's office. She was no beauty queen. But I could tell she came from good stock. Alexis never wanted children. She thought they would interfere with her social life. I thought Barbara and I could settle down and raise a family.

"When I told Alexis I was leaving her, she pleaded with me to stay. Then she threatened to take all my earnings. Luckily, I had enough money piled up to buy her off. For a while. When the money dried up, she started looking for other ways to squeeze this old lemon. Apparently, she had kept a lot of my old papers. She ran across the original manuscript of the short story with Lizzie Bogmire's name on it. I ended up telling her the whole, ugly truth.

"When you're a writer, being accused of plagiarism is worse than being accused of adultery, lechery, and ritual serial killings combined. People would forgive you for that. Not so with plagiarism. So when Alexis threatened to expose me if I didn't take her back, I felt I had no choice. She didn't even care if I kept Barbara on the side as long as we were discreet, and she got to keep up the pretense of being married to a neurotic, successful novelist. That was fourteen years ago."

"So you and Barbara never had kids?"

"Nope. Turns out, I'm a failure in that department. Just as well, now that I know she was only after the money, too. I sure know how to pick 'em." He scratched his head.

Deena sat on the side of her chair facing Max. "Obviously I don't know her like you do, but she doesn't strike me as a person capable of murder."

"That's what's so fascinating. Murderers don't all look like Cro-Magnons with big beards and jagged teeth. They look like you and me. But then, something happens that causes them to snap—or become desperate. Remember? I talked about this in class. Greed, revenge, lust, anger. It doesn't take much for some people to make a sharp turn to the dark side."

"You're right. I should know that by now. But to think someone you know has committed homicide..." She shivered. "How do you think she found out about your will?"

"She must have gotten my soon-to-be-ex-lawyer—her former boss—to tell her about it. Who knows, maybe she was having an affair with him on the side, too. Anyway, I was planning to leave my money to a charity that helps young writers in Austin and I was planning to set up a scholarship in Lizzie's name at the university. I'm such a coward, I couldn't see my way clear to do anything for Ms. Bogmire while I was still standing upright. I had hoped that by helping her when I was gone, I might atone for some of my sins and keep things a little cooler in the hereafter."

Deena wasn't sure how to respond. "Wow." Not very elegant, but the best she could come up with. What a tale. "So, whatever happened with Lizzie Bogmire?"

"Never heard from her again. Not during the daytime, anyway. Occasionally, she still haunts me in my sleep."

Deena measured her words carefully. "What would you say if I told you that *I* know what happened to her?" Deena shielded the sun from her eyes so she could see his reaction.

"I would say you were confirming that this great big earth is actually just a very small world."

"She's dead." Deena paused as Max's head dropped to his chest. "But I know her sister, and so do you."

"What?"

"She lives here in Maycroft. Maybe it's time to make amends. It sounds like the story is going to get out anyway now that Barbara knows about Lizzie. Maybe you should tell Lizzie's sister what you did and apologize."

"You mean like the twelve-step program for plagiarizing authors."

Deena grinned. "Something like that. Maybe it will at least help you sleep at night."

* * *

DEENA DROVE SLOWLY around Dead Wally's Curve on her way home from Max's house. She told his defense team she would be willing to talk if it turned out he still needed her help. Hopefully, the police would eventually charge his ex-wife Barbara instead of him.

Max was genuinely surprised to learn that Lizzie Bogmire's sister was Betty Donaldson, the librarian and student in his class. Deena had explained to him Betty's reaction when the three women had seen him kissing Barbara that day they had come by to bring food. He admitted that he was the one to call the police and report having seen her. He had not seen the other two women with her.

He was unsure that Betty would welcome a call from him under the circumstances. After all, he was still under indictment for the murder of his ex-wife.

Somehow, as usual, Deena had volunteered to talk to Betty on Max's behalf, not to tell her about the book but to explain that Max needed to tell her something.

She pulled up in front of Ian's office. Although she hadn't really done anything wrong, feelings of guilt crept up inside her. She got that from her father. She could remember him always apologizing to her mother for something or other. Deena had inherited his tendency to feel responsible for everyone and everybody.

Shoot. If she could just mind her own beeswax, she might not get herself into these sticky situations.

Rob once again welcomed her and walked her back to Ian's office.

"What have you done now?" Ian asked.

"You could at least let me sit down first. After all, I am paying you for your legal services."

"Not really. I figure that when you take over the thrift store for Sandra when the baby comes, it will be quid pro quo."

"Tit for tat."

"That's right. Now if you end up charged with a crime, we may have to renegotiate."

Deena held up her crossed fingers. "I think I'm good so far, but you never know."

Ian sat back and chuckled. "So what have you done since the last time we talked? Any more attempts on your life? I assume you're safe with Max Dekker charged."

"Well...about that."

"Uh-oh. Here it comes."

"I went to see him yesterday. At the jail."

Ian sucked in a deep breath.

She had grown used to people doing that with her. Gary, her editor, Ian. Only Russell seemed to understand her motivations. "I wanted to ask him why he tried to kill me."

"And you expected him to tell you?"

"No, not really, but I thought I could get a sense of his guilt or innocence."

"You realize that intuition doesn't mean a darn thing in a court of law. It's about facts."

"And in this case, they are all circumstantial. Even Guttman said so."

"So spill it. What did the accused say?"

"That he was innocent. That he was being framed."

Ian slapped the desk and leaned forward as if in a cartoon. "You're kidding! What a shock!"

"Very funny, counselor. Let me explain."

She went on to tell him about the encounter with Barbara Conroy and how the defense team thought Barbara was the guilty party. Ian listened intently, even taking a few notes. The more she talked, the more seriously he seemed to take her.

"So you've explained the clothes and the dirty handkerchief getting to the thrift shop and the motive of money. What about the attempt on your life? Did she think you were getting too close to the real killer?"

"Or too close to her money train. One or the other."

"What about the white car that followed you? Could she have been driving Max's rental?"

"That's what they are checking on. Max took her several places in it, so DNA inside will be of no use. They are trying to see if the mileage adds up to when Max remembers having driven it."

"That sounds a little flimsy. What about her alibi for the night of the murder?"

"Still waiting to hear back from Guttman. They didn't hold Barbara after she caused the commotion at the jail, and she's flown back home to New York. I'm also not sure how anxious Guttman is to prove his arrest was a mistake and to have a new case to prove."

"I hear that, especially one that is this high profile. Have you watched the news?"

"Last night. It's so strange to hear little ol' Maycroft mentioned on the national news stations." She hesitated but decided to go ahead and tell him everything, including the part about Lizzie Bogmire. "The thing is, it's about to get a whole lot stranger."

"What do you mean?"

"Sit back. I have a story to tell you about a thief, a book, and a big, fat lie."

Chapter 22

Deena's brain was bursting at the seams when she pulled onto her street in Butterfly Gardens. She loved the quietness of her little piece of heaven in the suburbs. Too bad she couldn't quiet the voice in her head. What could she say to Betty to convince her to go back to Max's house? Obviously, Max couldn't visit her at the library since he was being held by the long arm of the law, and his news wasn't something he wanted to deliver over the phone.

Max had said he really wanted the meeting to take place tomorrow so that his secret about Lizzie wouldn't hit the news before he had a chance to apologize to Betty.

Tomorrow. Was today Wednesday? Thursday? The past week seemed to have all run together.

As she approached the house, she was surprised to see the garage door up. Gary must have come home early for some reason. One of the things Gary took great pride in was the fact that they could actually park *both* of their cars in their garage, unlike most of their neighbors who kept at least one car in the driveway. Of course, it didn't hurt that Gary drove a small Mercedes.

As she got closer, she saw that her parking spot in the garage was taken. She suddenly felt violated, as though another woman were lying in bed next to her husband. She pulled in behind it and had a sinking feeling in her stomach.

Then it dawned on her. It must be Thursday, and her mother-in-law was here.

With all the distraction of the Dekker case, she had barely had time to think about Gary's birthday, much less cleaning her house for her in-laws. *Don't do it*, she thought, resisting the temptation to just pull out and drive off. *You can do this.*

She got out of her car, one foot at a time as if moving in slow motion. She took a deep breath and headed in through the garage.

Opening the door slowly, she listened for voices. All she could hear was the faint chatter of the television. Hurley barked and startled the bejeezers out of her.

Gary sat in his recliner and pushed down the leg rest when he saw her. He put his finger to his mouth and made a soft shushing sound. "Quiet. She's resting," he whispered.

Deena set her purse and keys on the entryway table and tiptoed like a cat burglar to the den. She motioned for Gary to follow her to the bedroom. She closed the door quietly behind them.

Gary opened the outside door to the patio to let Hurley out. "Where have you been?" he asked in a hushed tone.

Deena pulled off her jeans to find a more suitable outfit to wear for Mrs. Sharpe. "I was at Max Dekker's and then Ian's office. I forgot she was coming today. You might have mentioned it last night, you know."

"I just assumed you remembered. You *do* remember that we're having a party here on Saturday with lots of people coming, right?"

She shot him a look. "Duh."

Deena couldn't really be annoyed with him since she hadn't cooked, cleaned, or even bought him a present. One thing she didn't have to worry about was the cake. She just needed to slip out later and ask Christy Ann if she would make it on her own tomorrow. Maybe if Deena mentioned her mother-in-law, Christy Ann would be able to relate.

As she slipped into navy slacks and a soft coral sweater, a soft knock at the bedroom door caused them both to freeze. Suddenly, Deena was back in high school, and her father was about to catch her kissing her boyfriend.

Gary walked over and opened the door. "Mother, you're up."

"It was hard to sleep with all that racket." She looked across the room to the dressing area. "Deena, you're home. Finally."

Deena slipped on her loafers and then gave her mother-in-law an obligatory hug.

The elder Mrs. Sharpe looked down at Deena's feet. "I believe I wore those same shoes when I was a child." She turned and walked back to the den and sat on the sofa.

Deena and Gary followed.

"Gary, dear, would you mind fixing me a glass of iced tea?" She picked up a magazine.

"I'll get it," Deena said and hurried to the kitchen.

Gary walked up behind Deena and kissed her on the neck. She opened the cabinet. "It's gonna be a *long* weekend."

Chapter 23

The alarm rang bright and early Friday morning. Deena had a lot to accomplish. First, she needed to run up to the library to talk to Betty about Max. She dreaded it, but she was glad to get it over with early. Then, she needed to shop for party food, prepare the food, clean her house, buy Gary a birthday present—all while babysitting her mother-in-law.

Focus. She showered, dressed, and dried her hair as quietly as possible, hoping not to awake the sleeping giant.

When Deena came out of the bedroom, Mrs. Sharpe was already up and dressed. Her hair, the color of white frosting, was pinned in a neat bun on the back of her head. Her purple knit pantsuit looked like a Garanimals outfit they used to sell at Sears. She was piddling in the kitchen. "Would you like a cup of coffee, dear?"

Deena let out a sigh. "Sure." If her mother-in-law was going to take over her kitchen, she might as well let her serve her. "Milk and sweetener, please." She sat at the kitchen table and looked at the newspaper. The crossword puzzle had already been filled out.

"I took the liberty of cleaning out your refrigerator. I'd hate to see you or my baby boy poisoned by any of that spoiled food." Her reading glasses hung on a chain around her neck. "You really should pay attention to those expiration dates." She set a cup of coffee and a saucer on the table in front of Deena.

Deena had forgotten she even had those cups and saucers. She had gotten them as a wedding gift. Usually she just grabbed a large mug or an insulated travel cup.

"Next, I'm going to start on the pantry."

Deena didn't have the energy to argue. "Thanks," she mumbled, reading the front page of the newspaper. The main story was Dan's article about the murder case. No mention of Barbara Conroy or Lizzie Bogmire. She was relieved. Hopefully she could get Betty to speak to Max before the scandal broke about Max's plagiarism, although compared to a murder charge, it might not seem so shocking to anyone but Betty.

"Are you reading the story about Max Dekker? It's so fascinating. It even has your name in it as a possible second victim." Mrs. Sharpe placed another cup of coffee on the table and sat next to Deena.

The night before at dinner, Deena had told Gary and his mother all the latest about the Dekker case. The elder Mrs. Sharpe had been mesmerized. Apparently, she was a big fan of the writer and of mysteries in general. She seemed impressed that her daughter-in-law knew the big-time author and was helping him prove his innocence.

Deena had finally felt a kinship with the woman. It was short-lived, however, when Mrs. Sharpe made a catty remark about going out for dinner instead of Deena having prepared a meal. Of course, her food was too spicy, the service was too slow, and the restaurant was too dark. Besides that, she seemed to enjoy Deena's story. She thought it was despicable that he had put his name on someone else's story and vowed to write him a letter to tell him so.

"Are you going up to the library to talk to that Lizzie woman this morning?" Mrs. Sharpe asked as she finished re-reading the article over Deena's shoulder.

"Betty. Lizzie is her sister who passed away. But yes."

"I've been thinking," Mrs. Sharpe said. "Maybe whoever killed Mrs. Dekker killed the sister, too. Maybe Max Dekker killed her to keep her quiet."

Deena hadn't considered that angle. "Hmm. Like I said, I think Max is being framed. But maybe Barbara—no, Barbara didn't seem to know who Lizzie Bogmire was until she found out about the will. But still, maybe Betty will tell me the circumstances surrounding her sister's death."

"Do you want me to come with you?"

"I think it would be best if I spoke to Betty alone, but I appreciate the offer."

"All right. You seem to have a real knack for this investigative stuff."

Deena smiled and drank down the end of her coffee, relieved Mrs. Sharpe did not insist on accompanying her to the library.

"But I want to go shopping with you to buy food at the market. I can show you how to save Gary's hard-earned money, especially now that you aren't working."

And there it was. Just when she thought she could actually like the woman.

* * *

EXPECTING TO BE THE only person there, Deena was surprised to see a group of people milling around the library when she arrived at eight-thirty. A sign on the front counter read: "Genealogy for Beginners," and she immediately understood why she was the youngest visitor.

Betty was talking to an elderly couple by one of the computer stations.

Deena had always been interested in the topic and had once tried some of the ancestry sites online. Afraid she might uncover more relatives like her mother-in-law, she had taken a break from searching.

Nancy and Betty had overlapping shifts, so Betty was manning the place alone.

Maybe this wasn't the best time to do this, but for Deena, it was now or never. She caught Betty's attention and gestured toward the front counter.

Betty nodded and told the couple she would be back to help them in a while. "How are you doing, dear?" she asked, looking Deena up and down.

"I'm fine—thanks to you."

Betty dismissed the comment with a wave of her hand. "It was nothing. Are you here for more cookbooks?"

"What? No. I've given up on that. I'm here about you, actually."

Betty narrowed her eyes. "Me? Whatever for?"

"It's about Max Dekker. He wants to talk to you."

"To me? Why would that horrible man want to talk to me?" She glanced around the library at the busy seniors.

"He's really not that bad when you get to know him."

"Get to know him? I hope I never lay eyes on him again. Why would I want to talk to someone who cheats on his wife, kills her, and then tries to kill my friend? You'd be best to stay away from him yourself, if you know what's good for you." Betty walked off toward the computers.

The last comment caught Deena's attention. It sounded more like a threat than a warning. She knew this wasn't going to be an easy sell, so she was ready to pull out the big guns.

A book about World War I lay on the counter. Deena picked it up and turned to an inside page and strolled over to Betty. She whispered casually, "It's about your sister."

"My sister?" Betty practically yelled.

"Shhh," Deena said. "We're in a library." She had always wanted to shush a librarian.

"But I—" Betty stopped, straightened her shoulders, and marched to the library office.

Deena followed. By the time she caught up to Betty, the woman's face had flushed to a bright red.

"I have no idea what this is about or how my sister could be involved, but I repeat—I have *no intention* of talking to that despicable man! I want you to stay out of my business and out of this library. You have no right to come in here and start stirring things up, especially after all I've done for you. You are nothing but a busybody. Everybody in town says so. Now get out and don't come back!" She waved her arm, pointing toward the door.

Deena felt the color drain from her face. Her eyes watered as she turned to leave. She hurried out the door and got in her car. By the time she started the engine, the waterworks had begun to flow.

She had never upset someone so much in her life. All she wanted to do was help, but it was obvious Betty was hurt.

I should have minded my own business. Deena covered her face with her hands. She hadn't realized that her sister's death had been so hard on Betty. But she should have known. And then to bring up Max Dekker in the same conversation. Deena already knew Betty despised him. She reached in her glove compartment for some tissues and blew her nose.

She wanted to go back in and apologize. Deena hated loose ends and wanted to tie this one back up and make it right. She looked at her mascara-streaked face in the mirror. Betty wasn't ready to hear her apology. She knew that. Hopefully, when the time was right, Betty would be more forgiving of Deena than she was of Max Dekker.

How was she going to face her mother-in-law like this? What would she say? Deena drove around town wishing she had never gotten out of bed.

Betty's reaction was downright visceral. Why was she so hateful when it came to Max Dekker? Could she really be so angry just because she saw him kiss the other woman?

She thought back to their conversation that day in the library. Betty had seemed smitten with Max. She had arranged to have him teach the class. She made him a casserole and gave him all those cookies, for goodness sake. Now she wanted nothing to do with him. Could it be that somehow Betty found out what he had done to her sister?

It was another blustery day in Maycroft. The trees were dropping their leaves and blanketing the lawns of Butterfly

Gardens with Mother Nature's colorful quilt. Deena couldn't see the beauty. To her it felt like the world was conspiring to smother her under the weight of the wet blanket.

At last, she headed home. She parked in the driveway and prepared to face the music.

"What on earth happened to you?" Mrs. Sharpe asked. "You look like you lost your best friend."

Deena rubbed her swollen eyes. "Not my best friend, but a friend nonetheless."

Mrs. Sharpe took off the yellow plastic gloves she was wearing to work in the kitchen and engulfed Deena in a tight hug. "Now, now. It'll all be okay. This too shall pass."

Deena stiffened, unaccustomed to physical contact with Gary's mother. However, those last few words brought on a familiar feeling. Gary often said the same thing to comfort her. She relaxed in the woman's arms. Maybe her husband got some of his capacity for kindness from his mother after all.

"Now just sit down over here, and I'll fix you a nice cup of hot tea." She led Deena to the kitchen table.

Deena didn't want to say that she'd prefer another cup of coffee. "Thank you," she said. Who knows, maybe hot tea did indeed offer some healing power, like chicken soup or a salt-water gargle.

Mrs. Sharpe busied herself filling the dusty, rarely used teakettle that Deena kept for decoration on the stove. "Was that Lizzie woman mean to you? Do you want me to talk to her?"

"Betty," she said. "Yes, but it was probably my fault. I brought up her sister, and it obviously caused her a lot of pain. That's when she yelled at me." Deena felt like a little girl telling her mother about the schoolyard bully. "She said she didn't want me to ever come back to the library again."

"Well now, that's just silly. It's a public library. You have just as much right to be there as anyone." She set a teacup and saucer on the table.

Deena dabbed her eyes with a tissue as she thought of the stinging words Betty had used. "She also said I was a busybody and that everybody in town agrees."

Mrs. Sharpe stamped her foot. "Now that's simply not true. Just because you try to help people doesn't make you a busybody." The teakettle whistled, and she brought it over with a tea bag she must have found in the back of Deena's pantry. "Why, Gary tells me all the time about how brave you are and proud he is that you stand up for other people. If she doesn't understand that, well then she can just go jump in the lake."

Deena giggled. It warmed her to be defended for a change. She had never dreamed that Gary bragged about her to his mother. The aroma of the brewing tea did its magic. Deena stirred slowly and relaxed.

Mrs. Sharpe brought a cup for herself and sat down with Deena. "This Lizzie–I mean Betty—sounds like a real piece of work. She's saving your life one minute, and then biting your head off the next. Sounds like a crazy woman to me."

Smiling, Deena blew into her cup and took a sip. She relished the hot brew traveling down her insides, filling a place in her soul she hadn't realized was empty.

Mrs. Sharpe set down her cup. "I wouldn't be surprised if she comes from a long line of crazies. After all, who has two daughters with the same name?"

Tilting her head, Deena asked, "What do you mean?"

"Back in my day, no one was named Betty or Lizzie." Those were both just nicknames. Shortened versions of Elizabeth."

Deena took another sip of tea. She thought for a minute. Then a chill came over her despite the warm tea. Goosebumps popped out on her arms. It seemed she had a clear head for the first time in two weeks. She sucked in a deep breath and shivered.

"Are you all right, dear?"

"I've got to go," Deena said and leaped out of the chair. "I'll explain later." She grabbed her purse and keys off the entry table and dashed out to her car.

Betty Donaldson just *thought* she had seen the last of Deena.

Chapter 24

Why hadn't she thought of it sooner? Obviously, Betty had been obsessed with Max Dekker. She had practically blackmailed the woman at the college to get her to set up the writing class. Had Betty planned at that point to kill Max or was she really after his wife?

Deena's mind went back to that first day in class. Betty had been late because she had gone home to get supper. But when it was time to serve Lydia's cookies, she said she was starving. For a woman who was so thin and gaunt that she could walk between the raindrops, it was doubtful she could pack away much food. That must have been when she went to the salon to cut Alexis's brake line. Plus, she obviously knew her way around cars. She proved that the night she supposedly saved Deena's life.

Cookies. Betty had taken that big stack and put them on the desk for Max. That must have been when she dropped the greasy handkerchief in his briefcase. She had been wearing little plastic gloves like they wear to serve food in the school cafeteria. And Deena just thought Betty was being precautious because of germs. *That sneak!*

Deena pressed down harder on the gas pedal, blinding rage taking over her good sense. The closer she got to the library, the more convinced she was that Betty had killed Alexis Dekker.

So why try to frame Max for his wife's murder and then take him a casserole? Maybe to pretend to care about him? Deena would have to get that answer from Betty before she wrung her neck. The streetlight turned yellow at Main and Crawford, and Deena punched it. She pulled into a spot near the front door and leaped out of her car.

Inside, the genealogy group was gone. In a back corner sat the Pee Wee Story Time Circle. A group of small children listened as a woman read aloud.

No sign of Betty.

Deena stormed over to the front counter and banged repeatedly on the little metal bell.

Betty came out from the back, her usual sour face more puckered than normal. Seeing Deena, her eyes widened and her mouth dropped.

"It was you, wasn't it?" Deena scowled across the counter, pointing a shaky finger. "How *dare* you play the self-righteous martyr when you knew all along you were guilty!"

A shushing sound arose from the back of the library. Deena turned to see the whole group of mommies and their children admonishing her. When she turned back around, Betty was gone.

Deena raced around the counter into the back office.

Betty stood by a tall file cabinet trying to unlock it.

Balling her fists, Deena said, "Admit it! I want to hear you say it."

Betty's hand shook as she tried to aim the key into the small hole. "Now dear, I don't know what you think I have done, but I can assure you—"

Deena rushed toward her and grabbed at the key, knocking it to the floor. "Murderer! You killed Alexis Dekker and tried to frame Max. Then you went after me."

Betty threw an elbow at Deena and picked up the key. "You're insane!" The cabinet clicked open, and she reached down to pull open the bottom drawer.

Deena banged it shut with her foot. "Liar! I know who you are, *Elizabeth Bogmire*. That was your maiden name, right? The name you used when you wrote that short story back in college."

Betty turned around slowly and glared at Deena. Her expression had changed. Her dark eyes and stiff lips revealed a look that was both maniacal and amused. "So you figured it out. Well, good for you."

"Will you two hold it down in here?" It was a woman from the reading circle. "You're scaring the children."

"Good!" Betty shouted. "I hate those kids anyway."

The woman gasped.

"Call the police!" Deena yelled. "Call 9-1-1."

The woman turned on her heels before she was able to see Betty cold-cock Deena with a stapler to the back of her head.

Deena stumbled forward but caught herself on the desk. She picked up a three-hole punch and swung it like a bat toward Betty who managed to duck just in time.

"I should have let you die, too! Then Max Dekker would be in prison, and you wouldn't have gotten in my way." Betty charged at Deena, pushing her backward toward the laminating machine. Deena's right arm pressed against the hot roller, and she let out a scream.

But then her short stint at karate class kicked in. Tears blurred her vision as she swung her leg around to kick her attacker. She was surprised when her foot made contact with Betty's shoulder. Deena didn't know she could get her leg that high. Must have been the extra adrenaline.

Betty flew backward, knocking a large computer monitor onto the floor. Bits of glass and plastic sprayed her legs like shrapnel as she landed on the hard linoleum. She crawled toward the back exit, trying to push open the heavy glass door.

Deena reached for a book off the rolling cart and hurled it at Betty. "Here! Shelve this, you old witch!" She grabbed at the books, throwing them like grenades as Betty tried to bat them away. A particularly large cookbook met its target, hitting Betty square in the face.

Betty reached up and grabbed her bloody nose just as the sirens sounded and flashing lights flickered outside the back door.

The officers rushed in to find Betty crumpled on the floor, and Deena holding a dictionary. "Well, this is a fine mess," the officer said.

Deena recognized him from the night her brake line had been cut. "Arrest her, officer," Deena said as she gasped to catch her breath. "She killed Alexis Dekker and then tried to kill me."

IT TOOK A WHILE TO sort things out. The police hauled both Deena and Betty to the station. Ian came and sat with Deena while she gave her statement.

Luckily, the woman who called the police had stepped back into the office in time to hear Betty's confession. Her testimony sealed Betty's fate and corroborated Deena's story.

According to Detective Guttman, Betty had no remorse for her crime and even bragged about the details once she realized she'd been caught—hook, line, and sinker.

Detective Guttman insisted that Deena be checked out at the hospital before she returned home. The burn on her arm was pretty bad, and from the looks of the bump on the back of her head, she might have a concussion.

That took another hour or so, although Deena had lost track of the time. She had left her purse and cellphone in her car at the library, so she borrowed Ian's phone to call Gary. As usual, Gary was in a meeting, so she left a message for him to call Ian.

As a nurse wrapped her arm in gauze, someone pulled back the examining room curtain and stepped inside. It was Dan.

Deena couldn't believe it. He must have charmed his way to the back of the emergency room. "How did you know I was here?"

"I heard on the police scanner there was a disturbance at the library, and I had a feeling you'd be involved." He touched the side of his nose. "I've always told you I can smell a news story from miles away. So who won the fight, you or Betty Donaldson?"

"I think I did."

"That's my girl." He sat in a chair. "Of course, you may have won the battle, but there's still a war going on out there. There are a lot of Betty Donaldsons, and that's why you need to come back to work at the newspaper. You can help trap these rats and keep the mean streets of Maycroft safe and sound."

"Dan, don't be so cynical. Maycroft is a great place to live. Unfortunately, there are some people who fall prey to evil, but to say the place is crawling with rats? That's a bit much, don't you think? I mean, Betty wasn't always like this, I'm sure."

Dan crossed his legs and brushed dirt off the side of his boot. "Like Mark Antony said, 'The evil that men do lives after them. The good is often buried with their bones.'"

Always the teacher, Deena corrected him. "*Interred*, not buried. If you're gonna quote Shakespeare, at least get it right. You don't want to be accused of plagiarism, after all."

* * *

WHEN DAN DROPPED HER off at the house, Gary was just pulling in. He opened the car door to help her out. "I talked to Ian. Are you okay?"

"Yes, just a little bumped and bruised—and burned."

Gary stuck his head around the car door. "Thanks for bringing her home."

"No problem," Dan said. "See you tomorrow at the party."

Gary shut the car door and led Deena by the shoulders. "You invited him to my birthday party?"

"It just kinda came out."

"You know I'm not going to lecture you about all of this now, but don't think we're not going to talk about it later," Gary said, opening the front door.

"I know." She walked straight to the kitchen table and sat down, resting her arm on the table so Hurley wouldn't scratch it as he jumped. "You realize that I found the killer, right?"

"I do. How did you figure out it was Betty Donaldson?"

"It was actually something your mother said about Betty's name. By the way, where is your mother?"

"Maybe she's resting." Gary disappeared down the hallway. When he came back, his face was pale. "She's not there, but her car was in the garage, right?"

"Check the backyard," Deena said. After what she'd just been through, she had lost the energy to panic.

Gary hurried to the patio. "She's not there either," he said, his voice cracking. "What should we do? Call the police?"

Deena got up and walked toward the kitchen, spotting something on the counter. It was a piece of paper. She doubted it was a ransom note. The kidnappers would have willingly returned her mother-in-law by now. Deena read it aloud. "'At the neighbor's house making coke.'" She looked up at Gary. Now she was worried. "Making coke? Like cocaine? Do you think she's at Ed's house next door? I should have guessed he was a drug dealer!" She started toward the door.

Gary grabbed the note from her hand. "This doesn't say coke—it says *cake*. She's making a cake."

Deena smile sheepishly. "Ohhh. That makes more sense. She must be at Christy Ann's."

Gary held Deena's arm as they crossed the street. Christy Ann's five-year-old son answered the door. "Mommy, that lady is here!" he yelled and shut the door in their faces. Christy Ann returned, her blonde locks perfectly coifed. She wore a cute, ruffled apron. "Come on in, you two. Sylvia and I were just finishing up."

Deena glanced at Gary and then followed Christy Ann. It was only the second time Deena had been inside the dragon's lair. It was messier this time, with kids' toys strewn everywhere. The TV blared, and the three children seemed to be competing for their mother's attention. The baby won. Christy Ann picked her up and put her in a highchair in the kitchen.

The aroma of sweet baked goods filled the room. Mrs. Sharpe sat at the kitchen table cutting up a mound of fresh fruits and vegetables. "Well, look who decided to finally come home. After we made the cake—you know, the one you said you could bake yourself with no problem—we decided to work on the party food over here. That was several hours ago."

"But I—"

Gary came to the rescue. "Mother, Deena has been at the hospital."

His mother turned and stared at Deena's bandaged arm. "Oh dear. Bless your heart. Come sit down. Are you all right? Do you need anything? Were you in an accident in that big fancy car of yours?"

Christy Ann brought Deena a glass of iced tea. "Oh my. Your hair is a mess. What happened?"

It seemed Christy Ann and Sylvia Sharpe were two peas spawned from the same pod. "I'm fine." She took a sip of the sweet elixir. "I got in a fight with Betty Donaldson at the library."

"Like a fist-fight?" asked Christy Ann, her nose wrinkled with disgust.

"It was more of an office-supply fight." Deena proceeded to tell the whole story while Christy Ann dashed back and forth between the kitchen and the family room. Christy Ann already knew a surprising amount of information about the case, courtesy of the Maycroft gossip mill.

By the time Deena told them about how she had put the clues together and reenacted the fight scene, the vegetables and fruit were chopped, the homemade dips were prepared, and there were four dozen freshly baked cookies packed up in little tins. The only thing left was the big cake reveal.

When Christy Ann pulled the cover off the cake plate, there sat a perfectly delicious-looking chocolate swirl cake garnished around the bottom with white, fluffy divinity clouds.

All Deena could say was, "What?"

"You don't like it?" Christy Ann asked, sticking out her bottom lip.

"Oh, it's not that. In fact, it's beautiful. It's just not what I had envisioned at all."

"What *ever* do you mean, child?" Mrs. Sharpe asked.

Deena's eyes darted back and forth between the cake and her mother-in-law. Had this been a trick? "I thought the recipe said to put the divinity *in* the cake, not *on* it. Where's that card?"

Christy Ann presented her with the recipe and smirked. "Looks like someone needs some reading glasses."

Mrs. Sharpe let out a boisterous laugh. "Can you even imagine?" She turned to Christy Ann as if they were sharing a private joke. "Honey," she said to Deena, "maybe you better just stay out of the kitchen and stick to solving mysteries. I'm surprised you haven't burned down the whole house!"

Chapter 25

Gary's sister and her family arrived early. Gary manned the grill on the patio. Deena helped Mrs. Sharpe set out the food.

Christy Ann and her kids were the first of the non-family guests to arrive. Her husband, Parker, was still on the golf course and would be joining them later. She gave Deena quick air kisses and went straight to Mrs. Sharpe, hugging her shoulders. "Sylvia! You look so pretty today."

The two older children had on their swim trunks and floaties. They barely stopped long enough to put down their towels before jumping in the pool. They seemed oblivious to the fact that the water temperature had dropped over the past week.

"Who's minding the store?" Deena asked Sandra when she and Ian arrived.

"My niece is there today with one of her friends. I wouldn't miss this party for the world." Sandra glowed in her maternity sundress, and Ian looked more relaxed than usual. "I want to hear all about your pounding of Betty Donaldson. You know I never liked her."

Deena shook her head. "Oh, bless her heart. Hate can do mighty strange things to a person's mind. Before that, though, I want to hear what Ian found out from Guttman."

"Me, too," Mrs. Sharpe said, hooking her arm through Deena's. She had sneaked up behind them. "Better make it quick. *We* have more guests to greet."

Deena smiled. "Yes, *we* do."

"Betty sang like a canary," Ian said. "She even confessed to putting the GPS tracker on Deena's car. Apparently, she had bought it to keep tabs on her husband but had switched it over to your car when Lydia told her you were going to the cops. She said you were being too nosy for your own good."

"Did she say why she went over to Max's house with a casserole? Was she planning on poisoning him?" Deena asked, still confused about that point.

"Betty told Guttman that it had been her sick dream all along to see Max lose something he cherished and then have to pay for it. She thought it was the price he should pay for stealing her story and her chance to be rich and famous."

"So that must be why she wanted us to take food to him. She wanted to witness his grief for herself. No wonder she was so mad to see him standing there kissing another woman instead."

"Why didn't she just sue him?" Sandra asked. "That's what everyone else does."

Ian shook his head. "Because she had no proof. He had the only copy of the story."

"So Barbara Conroy had nothing to do with the murder then," Deena said.

"That's correct. Guttman got in touch with her. She was still in New York at the time of the murder. She also said she was the one who picked up the greasy handkerchief from Max's desk and threw it into the boxes of clothes she took to the thrift store."

"Did Betty say why she stopped me from driving my car after she went to the trouble of cutting my brake line?" Deena asked.

Ian nodded. "She said that after Max was arrested, she thought you wouldn't still be a problem. I guess you proved her wrong."

"Another mystery solved," Mrs. Sharpe said.

Sandra put one hand on Deena's shoulder and patted her own belly with the other. "This baby is going to have the smartest godparents in all of Maycroft."

"Me and Gary?" Deena asked wide-eyed.

"Of course! Now don't start being a dim-wit or else I'll change my mind."

Deena thought her heart would explode as she gave her friend a big bear hug, being careful not to squish the baby.

Just then, Russell and Estelle came through the front door with Cliff right behind them. He was leading someone by the hand. "Deena," he said, "I'd like you to meet my girlfriend, Rosemary."

At that moment, she knew this day couldn't get any better.

* * *

THAT EVENING AFTER all the partygoers had left, Deena plopped down on the sofa to enjoy the blissful sound of quiet.

Gary sat down beside her and put his arm over her shoulders. "Thank you for the great party. Best ever."

"You should thank your mother, too."

As if on cue, Mrs. Sharpe strolled in from the hallway. "I think I'm going to bed. It's been a tiring day, especially with your sister's family here. I mean to say, I love my grandchildren, but they can be *so* exhausting. That's why I enjoy coming here where it is so calm and peaceful."

Deena couldn't believe what she was hearing. "But I thought you hated it that we didn't have children."

"I never said that. I was sad for you two, of course, but some children need to learn to be seen and not heard, like back in my day. Well, goodnight all."

Deena was shocked. All this time she thought her mother-in-law resented her for being childless.

Before Mrs. Sharpe left the room, she offered up one more dig. "And Deena, dear, you really shouldn't ask Gary to help you clean up. After all, you did make him cook at his own birthday party."

Deena bit her lip and nodded.

After his mother was safely out of sight, Gary whispered in Deena's ear, "I think you two are bonding."

She laughed and then covered her mouth to stifle the sound. "She's not all bad, I suppose. She did raise an incredible son."

"Who chose an incredibly brave woman to marry."

"Brave or dumb?"

"You tell me?"

Deena paused to consider the question. "Did you know that Ian offered me my old job back as an investigator for his law firm?"

"Are you serious? In the course of two weeks, you went from unemployed to having two job offers. First, as a crime reporter and now, as an investigator." He scratched his head. "I think I like the idea of your being safely behind the counter at the thrift store over either of those two options."

Deena turned to face her husband. "I don't want to spend the rest of my life sitting in a rocking chair on the porch. That's not really a life."

"So what are you thinking? Do you want to go back to work at the newspaper?"

"After talking to Dan and seeing how cynical the job has made him, I don't think so. On the other hand, Ian still has such a big heart for people. He said he needs someone like me who shares his desire to help others. With Ian, it wouldn't be a full-time job. He would just ask for my help on certain cases. I could still run my antique business and maybe even tackle that mystery novel."

"And learn to cook," Mrs. Sharpe called out.

Deena turned to see her mother-in-law's head sticking out from around the corner in the hallway.

"I'll teach you myself. It will be fun." She took a few steps closer. "You wouldn't mind if I stay here with you two for a while, would you?"

Deena turned slowly back toward Gary, her eyes big as saucers. "It's going to be a *long*, *cold* winter."

THE END

Want to continue to continue reading the series? Check out
Sharpe Point: Needle in a Haystack, book 5.

SOMETIMES IN-LAWS ARE WORSE THAN OUTLAWS.

RETIRED FROM TEACHING, rookie investigator Deena Sharpe wants justice for the wrongly accused. She also wants to impress her new boss. But when she trips over a dead body in the church's haunted house, the police try to pin it on one of their clients. Can Deena defend a person she thinks may be guilty?

To make matters worse, Deena's mother-in-law has moved in and has plans of her own. She's determined to teach her son's wife how to properly cook and clean. But a clash with a nosy neighbor over the family's dog sends everyone into a tailspin.

Now, Deena must risk her reputation to sort through the secrets and lies of small town politics. However, when clues point to the pastor, his wife, and his secretary, she is stuck in the middle of an unholy murder case.

Sharpe Point, Book 5 in the Cozy Suburbs Mysteries, is a clean whodunit with plenty of snarky humor and a touch of romance. Buy it today to join in the fun.

Works by Lisa B. Thomas

COZY SUBURBS MYSTERIES
Sharpe Shooter: Skeleton in the Closet
Sharpe Edge: Stranger on the Stairs
Sharpe Mind: Hanging by a Thread
Sharpe Turn: Murder by the Book
Sharpe Point: Needle in a Haystack
Sharpe Cookie: Two Sides to Every Coin
Sharpe Note: Sour Grapes of Wrath
Sharpe Image: Danger in the Darkroom (Prequel Novella)

* * *

KILLER SHOTS MYSTERIES
Negative Exposure
Freeze Frame
Picture Imperfect

Dedication

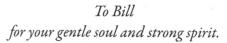

To Bill
for your gentle soul and strong spirit.

* * *

Acknowledgements

Thanks to all the readers who encourage me to keep writing. I feel your support every time I sit down to write.

A special thank you to my beta readers, especially Lia London. My editor, Kelsey Bryant, did a great job as well. Thanks also to Susan at coverkicks.com for the beautiful design.

Most of all, love and thanks to my husband for making it possible to pursue my dreams.

Made in the USA
Lexington, KY
20 July 2019